HEART OF GLASS

A DARK AND WILD NOVELLA

ANNE ROMAN

LA NOIR MEDIA, LLC

For anyone who ever wanted to take charge of their own story.
Write it babe, just write it.

CONTENT WARNING

Please read the content warning list and choose wisely whether to continue reading.

This book deals with some heavy emotional subjects such as the death of a spouse, verbal and emotional abuse, teenage pregnancy, ptsd, murder, drugs, and violence that may or may not involve an ass-bomb. Yes, you read the correctly. I promise the guy deserved it.

Fun content warnings: This book is for a mature reader, 18+ only. It does have explicit sexual content and touches on subjects of BDSM. It is NOT a BDSM book.

CHAPTER 1

LEIA

I picked up the socks and candy wrappers with a sigh. No matter how many times I told my son, Jameson, not to leave his socks and trash in the living room, and to walk the five feet from the couch to his bedroom where the trash basket was waiting to be used, he never seemed to get the message. Part of me wanted to leave it there on the floor and make him pick it up when he came home, but I knew it was safer if I just did it myself and tried to talk to him— again, about his bad habit when he came home from school.

School. *Shit.* I glanced at the clock. Three o'clock. The school bus would stop at the corner three blocks away from our apartment building and Sarah would come home from school. It was a four-minute walk by the time I left the apartment and made it down the street to get her. The bus wouldn't wait over twenty seconds. I was going to be late. Again.

I may not have been late if I hadn't stopped to pick up the socks, which made me notice the candy wrappers hidden under the couch. And the beer bottles left on the coffee table. I wiped my hands on my leggings and sighed. I hadn't worked out yet either. Could I skip it and put in more time tomorrow? Would he notice?

My stomach clenched. I couldn't worry about that right now. I had to get to the bus stop. Maybe if I hurried, the bus driver would be behind schedule today and I wouldn't be *that* late.

I grabbed my purse and keys off of the counter.

The steps would count as a workout, right? They would if I jogged instead of walked. Yeah. I'd jog instead of walk. That would have to do.

I reached the bus stop, panting. I hated jogging. I hated the way it made my legs feel. Hated the way it made my lungs burn. I hated the sluggish beat of my heart in my ears. I enjoyed working out and lifting weights. But jogging had never been something I'd enjoy. *But it's the best way to burn calories.*

The bus wasn't there, and my heart raced, but not from cardio. Shit. I pulled out my phone to see if the school office had called. They always notified parents if a child wasn't picked up from their stop in time. No missed calls. That could be good or bad. There weren't any other parents on the block picking up their kids for me to ask, either. All the children in our apartment building were either too old for the required pickup age, or were too young. Sarah didn't really have any friends where we lived, but she never complained.

I heard the rumble of a diesel engine and glanced up, a weight lifting off my chest. The bus was coming. They had delayed it long enough for me to make it.

I smiled as I saw a bright, blonde head descend off the bus and come running up to me.

"Mommy!" She wrapped her arms around me and looked up with a grin.

I held her close and kissed her head. I loved these afternoon greetings. It was the best part of my day.

She grabbed my hand and we started the walk back to our apartment. My phone buzzed in my hand and I looked down at the timer that was going off. A reminder: Pick up medicine for Jameson. I sighed. One more thing to do before I could go home.

I looked down at Sarah. "Want to run to the store with me?"

Sparkling, blue eyes turned up at me. "Sure! Can I get a sucker?"

I laughed. "Yeah, you can have a sucker, but only one."

She grinned, pleased, and I squeezed her hand as we stopped at the city bus pickup, waiting for the one that would take us to the drop-off near the pharmacy. Hopefully, this wouldn't take too much time and I would be able to get back in time to start on dinner. I glanced at the time on my phone. 3:15 pm. I had two hours to get the medicine and get back home. That should be plenty of time.

I looked at my phone. 4:15 pm. It had been a full hour since I'd checked it at the bus stop. Sarah stood next to me, already on her second candy sucker, and was waving it back and forth like a magic wand. I pulled her closer to me so she didn't hit the handsome gentleman in the designer suit who was standing in line behind us with her candy.

When I'd gotten to the pharmacy, it had been short-staffed, as the nice lady at the counter had explained to me, and my medicine pickup wasn't quite ready yet.

"Oh, okay. Can you tell me how long it will take?" I'd asked, glancing at my phone again for the 100th time. It had been 3:30 pm. The lady had popped her gum and said, "We will have it ready as soon as possible. You can either wait or come back." I'd fidgeted, trying to decide. "I'll wait." She'd nodded and turned away.

Forty-five minutes later, I was still waiting, only now there was a line of people waiting with me. Including the guy in the expensive suit. The ridiculously, hot guy in the expensive suit. I glanced at him in the security mirror and blushed when I saw his eyes staring directly into mine. Gorgeous, aquamarine-colored eyes. He frowned, and I glanced away. Asshole guy in a business suit, apparently. What a guy like that, who clearly had enough money to have someone pick up his prescriptions for him, was doing at a run-down pharmacy like this, I didn't know. But I also knew I shouldn't be letting myself get distracted. I had to get home.

I approached the counter again.

"Umm, excuse me, do you think my prescription is ready yet? I really need to get home."

The lady looked up at me, blinking behind her neon green glasses. "Oh! Yeah, we finished it. I thought you'd already gone home." I frowned.

"I've been standing in line this whole time." I eyed the thickness of her glasses. Did she need her vision checked?

She shrugged, "Sorry, like I said, didn't see you." She began typing away on her computer and I handed her my ID and insurance card when she paused.

"Oh. It looks like your insurance isn't approving this medication. We can get you the generic version, but you'll need to come back tomorrow to pick it up." I flinched. Tomorrow would be too late. Jameson was already on his last pill and I hadn't had a chance to pick up a new prescription until now.

"I can't do tomorrow. How much is this one

without insurance?" Maybe the name brand wasn't too expensive and I could cover the cost upfront. I'd call the insurance company tomorrow to see if they would reimburse me.

"Three hundred and twenty dollars—." She popped her gum and blinked at me. "—and nineteen cents."

I began to sweat. Over three hundred dollars? For medication? There was no way I could afford that. I looked at the little green bottle of pills. My phone buzzed in my hand and I ignored it. Pay three hundred twenty dollars now, or come back tomorrow. My phone buzzed again, and I glanced down at the message.

Jason: "Hey, on my way home, early. Is dinner going to be ready on time today?"

Shit, shit, shit. My heartbeat pounded in my ears as the panic began to rise.

"Is there a problem?" A deep voice sounded from behind me and I nearly jumped out of my skin. Turning around, I felt my pulse skip several beats as I realized Mr. Expensive Suit standing mere inches from me. The harsh, fluorescent light glinted off his blue-black hair, and this close, I realized his eyes were a deeper blue than the aquamarine I'd originally thought. He smiled, and I had to refrain from gasping when I saw his white teeth flash. I don't think I'd ever seen a more beautiful man outside of movies or magazines.

Suddenly my racing heart had nothing to do with my tight timeline, and everything to do with the man who was too close to me. His cologne hit my senses, something spicy and warm that had me envisioning dark, leather chairs and crackling fires. I wanted to lean in closer to breathe him in. He even smelled rich. What the hell was wrong with me? There was something familiar about him as well, though I didn't understand why. How long had it been since I'd been this attracted to a man? Too long. Guilt made me shrink back. I had a fiancé. A fiancé I was thinking about breaking up with, sure, but I still shouldn't be thinking about the sexy, rich businessman wearing nothing but his cologne, leaning back in a leather Chesterfield as he sipped on a glass of whiskey, beckoning me towards him.... shit I was daydreaming again. This had to stop.

"Um, no. No problem." I stammered and

reached for Sarah's hand. "Come on baby, we need to go."

"But mommy what about Jamie's medicine? He needs it. I heard Papa Jason say you needed to get it today."

I swallowed. "Well, we can't get it today. We have to come back tomorrow."

"No, Mommy, you need to get it now!" She pulled her hand out of mine and ran back to the counter, pulling a wad of paper and coins out of her pocket. "Here Mommy, I have money. Buy it and then you won't cry and Papa Jason will be happy."

I flinched at her words, feeling my cheeks turn red-hot as the counter lady stared at me, and the eyes of the businessman bore into the back of my skull. "Baby, it's fine. We need to get home and get dinner. Jason is on his way now."

Sarah pouted, but grabbed her wad of paper and coins off the counter and slipped her hand into mine as I led her away.

A glance up at the security mirror told me the lady at the counter had gone back to typing on her computer and popping her gum. But the businessman with the beautiful, blue eyes was still watching as we walked away.

LEIA

Sarah and I made it home right before five o'clock. We'd had to run most of the block back to our apartment building, and I was going to count that as a second workout because, technically, I'd been carrying her.

Unlocking the door, I opened it to the TV blaring some anime show, sneakers, a backpack and a sports bag crowding the small entryway. I glared at the mess.

"Jameson!" I snapped my voice, raising it over the sound of the TV.

A dark, blonde head popped up over the couch. "Oh, hey mom. What's up?"

"Could you *please* pick up your stuff?" I

pointed to the mess as Sarah began removing her own backpack, jacket and shoes.

"Yeah, sure, in a second. I just want to finish this episode." He slid back down and turned around to the TV, I pinched the bridge of my nose and sighed. "No, Jameson, do it now, please."

"I will Mom, jeez, one second."

"Jameson Parker, now!" I snapped. One name was usually enough to make him move at a snail's pace. But when I used two names, he knew I meant business.

He jumped and glared at me, coming around the couch and into the entryway. "You know, for once, Mom, it would be nice to come home and have a hug or something other than getting screamed at."

I cringed, guilt twisting my gut. "Jameson, please don't start this. You know you can't throw your things down the minute you walk in the door."

A voice called from the kitchen, "Well, he wouldn't if you'd stop treating him like a baby and start treating him like a man. He probably gets his cleaning skills from you, anyway."

I deflated. I was home too late. Jameson

glanced at me with an apologetic expression and bent down to pick up his bag. "Sorry, mom." He whispered, "I forgot."

"I know baby, I know. It's okay. Just try to remember for next time."

Jameson was eleven and on the verge of puberty. He was a good kid, but often forgot to follow through with his tasks and daily chores. It was part of the reason he needed his medication today. Without it, the inattentiveness and lack of focus only doubled, making even the simplest task difficult for him to manage. I knew I'd be getting a phone call from his teacher tomorrow.

I made my way to the kitchen to see my fiancé, Jason, sitting at the table, a beer bottle already open and resting on the wood of my grandmother's antique kitchen table, condensation pooling around the bottom of the glass. I sighed and grabbed a coaster and rag. I bet the man in the expensive suit would never even think about putting a bottle of beer down on wood.

Jason huffed as I wiped up the mess and slipped the coaster under the bottle. "What's got your panties in a twist?" He narrowed his green eyes at me before glancing at the clock.

"I told you I was on my way home. Where

were you? Where's dinner?" It was after five now, and it took every ounce of self-control I had not show my frustration at his words.

"I was at the pharmacy picking up Jameson's medicine. It took longer than I thought." I didn't tell him I didn't get the medicine. It would only start an argument, and that was something I wasn't in the mood to deal with at the moment. Opening the refrigerator door, I pulled out the few ingredients I needed for tonight's dinner, setting them on the counter.

He stood up, following me into the kitchen, his hands coming to slip around my waist, his breath hot on my neck. I wrinkled my nose at the pungent scent of tobacco and sweat. Mr. Expensive Suit and his delicious-smelling cologne flashed through my mind. This was twice now that he'd crossed my thoughts in a matter of minutes. What was wrong with me? I tried to pull away gently, as the combined smell of beer and tobacco dip made my stomach sour. I'd never liked it. "Do you want to go take a shower?" I prayed he'd get the hint without getting offended.

Jason snorted, "What's wrong baby? Don't like the smell of a hard-working man?"

I willed my face to remain blank and not show

any emotion while I calmly kept cutting the vegetables that were going to go in the oven to roast for dinner. "No, I just thought you'd like to relax and clean up before we ate."

He frowned, taking a swig from his bottle as if he was suspicious of my words, before nodding. "Yeah, you're right and maybe when I get out, you'll be in a better mood and not such a bitch. You know, you used to be excited to see me when I came home." He turned around and stalked toward our bedroom. The door slammed shut, vibrating through the tiny apartment and I flinched at the sound. I tried to calm the racing of my heart.

Things hadn't always been this way between us. There was once a time when I'd thought he'd been the answer to my broken and grieving heart. He'd been there for me at some of the darkest times of my life. But now it was like I lived with a stranger. A stranger I couldn't escape. Not yet, at least. But soon. I'd found a resource recently for women and children who needed help to leave difficult situations. But I hadn't worked up the courage to contact them yet.

I peeked over the counter into the living room

where Jameson and Sarah were cuddled up on the couch together, watching a kids show.

I had just turned seventeen when I found out I was pregnant with Jameson. My boyfriend, Danny, had been amazing. When other guys his age would have run off or abandoned their girl-friends, he'd stuck by me the entire time. He'd joined the military as soon as he turned eighteen and we'd gotten married shortly after.

The first few years had been rough. But we'd worked through it. I'd gone back to school for my GED, then applied for college and earned my degree in marketing and communications. I was hired on right away to an up-and-coming media company, and quickly fell in love with my job. Soon after I started working, I became pregnant with Sarah and our family grew again. Danny found success at his job too, and had quickly been promoted through the ranks of the Army. Military life wasn't easy. Danny was gone a lot and the kids and I missed him. Balancing being a single mom while Danny was deployed was difficult. But we'd made it work and had been happy.

Life can turn upside down so fast though. What had once been a modest, fairytale life had ended in heartache and grief. Danny deployed on his scheduled rotation and never came home. One minute he was there— his boots by the door, his keys hanging next to mine, and the next, I was receiving a folded flag and being offered condolences from men and women I hardly knew. All friends of Danny's. All strangers to me.

That's when Jason stepped in. He'd been one of Danny's best friends and was the one person I was the most familiar with. It was almost as if Danny had never left. Jason bonded quickly with Jameson and Sarah, becoming the father figure they no longer had.

Still, my heart wouldn't let Danny go.

It had taken a while, but eventually, Jason had worn down my walls and convinced me that we could be a family. That my children deserved to have a father in their life. He'd asked me to marry him one year after Danny's death and I said yes. It was almost impossible for me not to. The kids loved Jason and, if I was being honest, it was nice to have someone else to rely on and share the parenting load.

For a while, we'd been happy. We were a family again. Life was perfect. Jason and I began planning our wedding and life together, even though it was painful and the memory of Danny had never truly faded.

But then things slowly changed. The fairytale I tried to dream up, turned into a nightmare.

It was little things at first. Jason convinced me that the kids deserved a mom who was home with them. He told me that he was all the provider they needed and that he'd take care of us. And I loved that idea. I'd always struggled with balancing my success as a businesswoman and being a single mom. The guilt and his insistence drove me to give up my corporate job, and he'd moved in with us.

At that time, he'd still been on active duty like Danny, but then he'd gotten out, choosing not to renew his enlistment. The wedding had to be postponed, but he wasn't phased by it. We were going to get married and it was all going to be ok. He'd reassured me, charming me with dazzling plans for the future and the life we were going to build together. And I'd believed him. He told me he was going to start a business and we'd be making money hand over fist. All he needed was some collateral. So I'd used some of the life insurance money paid by the military from Danny's death to help fund the start-up.

Things had been great for a while after that. But I should have known it wouldn't last. I should have seen the writing on the wall. Because suddenly the business dried up and the investors came calling, wanting their money back, only the money was all gone. The business was bankrupt.

Jason begged me to help. Swore it was all someone else's fault and that he'd been tricked into making a bad investment. And I believed him once more, because that's what you did when you loved someone. You believed in them and supported them no matter what.

We'd move back to his hometown, where he had connections and people he could trust. We'd start over with a new business and a new plan, and it would be so much better. I'd clung to that hope that everything would be "better" as I sold my home, everything I owned that didn't have sentimental value, and moved across the country from North Carolina to Wild, Colorado. By the time the last box was taped up and loaded onto the moving truck, I'd convinced myself that this was what we needed. The kids and I needed a new place, a fresh start and distance from the memory of losing Danny.

It took even less time for the investors and

debt collectors to come collecting when Jason failed to follow through with his newest venture. And instead of a five-bedroom house and big backyard in a neighborhood full of kids and other families like we'd moved away from, we ended up here. In a tiny, two-bedroom apartment on the outskirts of a city that seemed to take its name to heart. Wild, Colorado. Shortly after Jason accepted the only job that was available, working at a machine shop, I became a woman who no longer recognized herself in the mirror.

I was a fool.

It wasn't long after we moved into the apartment that he started cutting me down. Word by word. Bit by soulful bit.

I wasn't cooking enough, or my cooking skills weren't up to par. He worked hard. Didn't he deserve a good, home-cooked meal?

The kids left too many messes. I needed to clean more, and it was my job since I was the stay-at-home parent while he worked and paid for everything we had. He was only trying to establish order and discipline in the house.

Why didn't I work out more? We were going to be together for the rest of our lives and he kept his body in tip-top shape for me. Why wouldn't I do the same for him? I snorted, thinking about the cases of beer he drank nightly.

If I'd supported him more and helped him with his business, he wouldn't have failed. We'd be living the dream right now. It was my fault we were in the situation we were in.

The words he had spewed at me swirled in my head and I sighed, the sense of defeat over-whelming me. He wasn't always like this. But lately, the attacks had been coming at lightning speed, one after the other and I could never get a word in to defend myself. And when I did? I was crazy. How could I not see that he loved me and wanted the best for me and the kids? I'd known for a while that it was time to go. That I couldn't put the kids and I through any more of his anger and verbal, or emotional abuse. Everything in me told me it wouldn't be long before that abuse became more than just cuts into my mind and soul. I had to get out. But with no resources or friends in the city, I hadn't had the courage to walk away yet. But then I saw a flyer for the Wild One's Foundation, and deep down I knew the time was coming soon.

Pain lanced through my finger. "Shit." I looked down to see deep red blood welling up from a cut where the knife had slipped and sliced my finger.

Grabbing a paper towel, I wrapped it up and headed back to our bedroom and the master bathroom for a bandage.

Steam billowed out from the closed bathroom door, and when I turned the doorknob I realized he'd locked it. I knocked. "Jason! I need to get in. Can you open the door?"

Pressing my ear to the thin wood, all I could hear was the sound of the shower. "Jason! I cut my finger and need a bandage!"

I heard a muffled, "Jesus, Leia, can't a man get a minute? I'm almost done."

I sighed and sat down on our bed, holding the towel to my bleeding finger, the red seeping through. Peeling it back, I swore. It was deep. I might need stitches.

There was a vibration next to me and I looked down to see Jason's phone on the bed. A notification popped up, and the name made me frown. It was our neighbor, Heather. What was she doing texting Jason?

Curiosity got the best of me and even though I knew I shouldn't have looked, something twinged in the back of my mind and it was like my hand moved on its own, swiping the notification and entering the passcode to his phone.

Blood pounded in my ears as the world began to spin around me.

There, in the open chat on his phone, was our neighbor— completely naked, with her legs spread and only one hand covering her vagina. A message bubble popped up, and I stared at it as if I was watching from a distance. Words appeared.

> Baby G: "I saw you came home early, baby. Want to come over for dessert once she goes to bed?"

The door to the bathroom opened, and the steam hit me in the face.

"What the fuck are you doing with my phone?"

CHAPTER 3

RHETT

The woman in front of me with the child clinging to her side, had the sexiest legs in a pair of yoga pants that I had ever seen. Somehow, I knew that it wasn't the forced illusion of spandex that made her fill-out and stretch the cloth with curves in all the right places. I could make out the swoop of a muscled thigh and the flex of her calf, as she shifted her weight and pulled the girl closer to her. Something about a woman with curves like hers did something to me. A twinge of jealousy pierced through me as I eyed the little girl and realized she was probably married. Lucky bastard.

Inadvertently, I glanced up at the security mirror, saw her staring at me, and sucked in a breath as recognition hit. Fucking hell, what was *she* doing here?

I'd stopped in to one of the local pharmacy chains that my company owned. A habit I had developed during my time as an officer in the military when I would drop into my platoon's offices, solely to observe and assess the unit's performance. The brief inspections weren't meant to get anyone in trouble, but rather to keep tabs on the health of the company. A company didn't function if the lowest levels were suffering, and a lot of times the guys would keep their issues to themselves rather than bring it to their command team. After leaving the service to take over for my father, I'd found a lot of similarities between the way a business was run and the way the military taught me to operate as a commander.

Since branching out to Wild, Colorado, I'd yet to stop in and check on the newest additions to our chain of drugstores. But since personal matters had brought me to the city, I had taken time away to remedy the situation.

Never in a million years had I thought I'd run into *her*.

But there she was, Leia Morrow. Staff Sergeant Danny Morrow's widow.

When her blue eyes had met mine in the security reflection mirror for a moment, I thought she'd recognized me. But then she looked away almost as if she was avoiding my gaze, pulling the little girl who was standing next to her closer to her side.

Sarah. That was the girl's name. The last time I'd seen her, she'd been a toddler, sitting in Leia's lap and staring up at me with wide, blue eyes that looked exactly like her mother's. It had been the day of Danny's funeral, and I'd arrived from overseas just in time to conduct the ceremony and give the eulogy. Words that had sat like cardboard on my tongue. Words that I couldn't even remember now.

But I remembered her, Leia, and her gorgeous, blue eyes that had looked at me and somehow through me as I handed her the folded up flag. I'd never forgotten those eyes.

I looked around for the little boy who had been with her at the time, too. He'd been a couple of years older than the little girl. What was his name? Ah yes, Jameson.

I heard Leia's voice soften, and noticed the pharmacy tech behind the counter shaking her head with a visibly-irritated expression when I realized I had been staring at them without fully registering what was happening.

"Is there a problem?" I shouldn't have said anything. I should have let the tech handle it on her own. But something in me couldn't help myself from asking the question.

Leia turned around and stared at me, her eyes going wider as if she was on the verge of panicking. Her cheeks flushed and I couldn't help but think she looked prettier with color added to them. The woman in the mirror had looked pale and tired. Like a deflated version of herself. I cringed at the thought. This woman was a widow with two kids. Who was I to judge her appearance, or if she was tired or not? She probably was.

I thought maybe, judging from her blush, she would have recognized me at that point. But all she did was stammer something and pull her daughter away from the counter. But Sarah wasn't cooperating.

"But mommy, what about Jamie's medicine? He needs it. I heard Papa Jason say you needed to get it today."

The little girl pulled away from Leia and ran to the counter, dropping a few pennies and dimes onto the counter. *Papa Jason?* So maybe she wasn't a widow after all. Maybe she'd moved on and found happiness. Some part of me was relieved at the thought. But then Sarah spoke again and alarm bells went off.

"Here mommy, I have money. Just buy it and then you won't cry and Papa Jason will be happy."

I saw the way Leia flinched at her words, her eyes tightening, her throat swallowing nervously. I saw the way her hands shook as she grabbed Sarah's hand, swiftly pulling her towards the exit, and then they were gone before I had a chance to say anything else.

A snarl came out of no where, the reaction surprising the people closest to me, causing them to step away. That wasn't a sign of a happy and content woman.

Leia was afraid.

I moved to the counter, and the bored-looking pharmacy tech straightened when she saw me.

"How can we help you, sir?"

"The woman. What medicine was she trying to buy?"

"I'm sorry sir, that's confidential, I can't—"

I cut her off by pulling out my ID and pointing to the back wall where my picture hung next to my father's. "Do you know who I am?" It wasn't often that I used that card. It wasn't often that I needed to. I knew how to be an intimidating asshole when I needed to be. And in this business, more often than not, I needed to be. But I was aware that in this instance my last name would get me farther than scaring the piss out of the lady who was simply trying to do her job.

Her eyes went wide as she looked at my photo ID, before her focus shifted to the wall. "Oh my God, Mr. Barrett! Oh shit, yes sir, but I'm so sorry. I still can't tell you."

I smiled, and I knew it wasn't friendly, as the woman blinked at me with little beads of nervous sweat dotting her forehead. "It's ok," I glanced at her nametag. "... Penny. You don't need to tell me anything. Is the order still up on the screen? Just a yes or no, please."

Penny nodded. "Yes, Mr. Barrett. It is."

"Good. Good." I pulled out my card and slid it to her. "Ring it up. Don't worry about signing for anything. I'll have this delivered, signed and back here before the pharmacy closes."

Penny trembled as she took my card. "But Mr. Barrett, that's against company policy..." her voice trailed off as I leaned in closer to her.

"Do it now, Penny." My voice was nothing but

a sharp command. The kind of command that soldiers followed instantly and without hesitation. The kind of command that made my decisions in the boardroom final.

She stiffened and immediately began typing away at her computer, then ran the card and handed me both the prescription bag, and the paper that Leia would need to sign for the medication.

"Please Mr. Barrett, we close at 7:00 pm. I need that back before the end of my shift." Her eyes were pleading with me, and I nodded. I'd have it back.

It wasn't until I walked out of the pharmacy and onto the street that I remembered I had no clue where Leia even lived.

I pulled my cell phone out of my suit pocket and slid into the back seat of the blacked-out Cadillac SUV that was waiting for me.

I quickly typed out a message as the driver patiently waited for my directions. Within seconds, I had an answer. A small apartment building near a strip mall that was only a few blocks away. Giving my driver the address, I sat back and stared at the brown package with the single bottle of medicine inside. Three hundred dollars for medicine? Yes, it was steep, and I had honestly been shocked at the price myself. But I remembered Danny always bragging about how talented and successful Leia was. He'd planned to get out and work full-time as a carpenter because she would be the main breadwinner in the house.

Danny had never enjoyed military life. He'd been good at it, but that was because Danny was good at most things he put his mind to. It was being a dad that he truly loved, though. And Leia. He'd talked about Leia so much. It was like I knew her, too.

Or did.

The car came to a halt, and I got out with a word to the driver for him to wait. The building I stared up at made me frown. I'd expected something a little less rundown, considering what I knew about Leia and the money she would have gotten from Danny's life insurance settlement. Nevertheless, it was evident that something had dramatically changed in her life for her to end up here. Especially here in Wild. I couldn't remember Danny having ever mentioned living here before.

Taking the elevator up to the floor where their

apartment was, I reached the door just as I heard a crash and cursing coming from inside.

Immediately, I went on high alert and instincts took over as I shoved my shoulder against the door, but it didn't budge. I backed up to try again, but before I slammed into it again, the door was flung open and a gangly pre-teen boy— who was the spitting image of Danny, was staring me in the face.

"Who the hell are you?"

"Jameson! Language!" Leia's voice snapped and my eyes flew above the boy's head to see his mother come storming around from what must have been the kitchen. A bloody paper towel wrapped around her hand.

A man I instantly recognized, holding a towel around his hips with a nasty expression on his face, was charging after her. I saw the blood, saw his expression, saw the fear in Jameson's eyes and before I knew what was happening, I was charging my way inside and had Jason up against a wall, my forearm crushing into his windpipe.

He sputtered and spewed as his eyes went wide with shock and recognition.

"Major Barrett? What the fuck are you doing here?" He choked out, and I pressed on his neck harder. My control was on a razor-thin edge. I chalked it up to seeing any woman in a situation like this, not just because it was Leia.

"I'd like to know what the fuck *you* are doing, Jason?" I glanced over at Leia, who was staring at me in utter shock and disbelief, but I didn't let go. "Leia, are you ok?"

She blinked, those large, blue eyes looking at me as if she was seeing a ghost. But she didn't speak, only nodded her head as if the words were caught in her throat.

I glanced down at her bloody hand and mentally counted to three before I lost all control and smashed my fist into Jason's face. He'd always been a nasty fucker, but I'd never have guessed that he'd do something like that. "Did he do that?" I nodded to the hand and again she remained silent, but shook her head no. Her eyes kept darting between me and Jason, as if she couldn't believe what she was seeing.

Satisfied, I slowly eased up on the pressure, staring into Jason's eyes. "I'm going to let you go and you're going to stay right fucking there. Do you understand?"

I could see Jason's mind mentally warring over whether to listen to my command or to tell me to fuck off. But old habits die hard and he nodded, "Yes, Sir."

"Good." I stepped back and turned back to Leia.

"Do you need to go to the hospital?"

"I…" her voice shook. "I think I need stitches."

Jameson and Sarah were huddled next to their mother, and a fierce protectiveness rose in me. I had no idea what I was doing here. I wasn't the hero or savior type. But I knew I wasn't walking away without them coming with me.

"Jameson, Sarah, I know you kids don't remember me, but I was a good friend of your dad's. I'm going to take your mom to the hospital to get her stitches and I'd like you both to come with us. Is that ok?" The kids wide-eyed stares flicked between me and their mother. I noticed they didn't once look at Jason.

"Now hold on a damn minute." Jason spoke, and I leveled a glare at him, but it was Leia who spoke.

"Yes, it's fine. Kids go grab an overnight bag. We won't be coming back." Leia wasn't looking at me, she was looking at Jason when she spoke.

Jason's face turned purple with rage, and he

took a step towards Leia. "Where the fuck do you think you're going?" I stepped between them, my face mere centimeters from his, and snarled.

"That's none of your business, Jason. She's going wherever she needs to go and I'll make sure she gets there. Back away before you do something you'll regret."

"That's *my* fiancé, Major, and you aren't in command of me anymore." If I was raging earlier, now I was seething. How had this low-life piece of shit convinced a woman like Leia to marry him?

I felt a hand on my arm and looked down to see her gently pushing me back.

"Not anymore Jason. We're done." She held a small, diamond engagement ring in her fingers and dropped it on the floor as the kids came racing around from their bedrooms with their bags.

I looked between her and the children. "Do you need anything else before we leave?"

It didn't matter. Whatever Leia needed, I would make sure she got. It was the least I could do for Danny.

She shook her head. "No, I just want to go."

Nodding, I waited until they'd walked out the door before I turned back to Jason.

"Do not call her. Do not follow her. Do not contact her ever again. Do you understand?"

He sneered, "You can try to come in here and play the hero, but you know nothing about Leia. She'll be back."

I didn't think. Didn't even try to reason with my actions as the next thing I knew, my fist was flying towards his face, blood bursting from his nose as he dropped to the ground.

"No. The fuck. She won't."

And then I left.

I didn't know how or why. But I knew one thing for certain. Leia Morrow was never coming back to this place again.

CHAPTER 4

LEIA

The kids stood next to me as we waited for the bus. Despite everything that had happened within the last thirty minutes, I was surprisingly calm. Seeing Mr. Expensive Suit from the pharmacy had been a shock, and hearing Jason speak to him like he'd been someone he knew had been even more shocking, but somehow, it didn't bother me. The only thing I cared about was that I was free. I looked down at Jameson and Sarah. *We* were free.

While I'd been already in the final stages of gathering the courage to tell Jason it was over, fear and guilt had still held me back. Jason wasn't the man I thought he was, and I'd known that for a long time now. But I'd been too scared to upset the kids and ruin the little bit of stability they had after Danny's death. I realized now that all I'd done was prevent us all from moving on with our lives. The thought sank like a stone in my gut. This was my fault.

Mentally, I was already calculating my next steps. I'd contact the Wild Ones Foundation, and as soon as we got to the hospital where I could get my finger taken care of.

I had a small amount of money stashed away that Jason had not been able to touch. It was supposed to have been for Jameson and Sarah's college fund. Something that Danny had insisted we start when they were only babies. I'd never told Jason about it and never planned to touch it, but it was all I had until I was able to get back on my feet. I knew in this instance, Danny would approve. It was a feeling that I hadn't experienced in a very long time. Like being wrapped in one of his warm hugs.

God I missed his hugs.

I heard footsteps and turned, half expecting to see Jason chasing after us. But it was Mr. Expensive Suit. No, Barrett. *Major Barrett.* The name seemed familiar and now that I was paying attention, so did he. He was scowling. "What the fuck are you doing, Leia?"

His rough language had me scowling right back. "Please don't curse in front of my children. And what does it look like I'm doing? We're waiting for the bus."

His eyes flicked from me to the bus stop sign as his frown deepened. "Leia, I told you I'd take you to the hospital, and I meant it. You don't need to take a bus."

Who was this guy that he said my name like he knew who I was? And what was it he'd said to the kids? That he'd been a friend of their father's? But I couldn't ever remember Danny talking about a Major Barrett. I shook my head. "Listen, I appreciate what you did back there, and your timing was impeccable. But I don't know you, no matter who you say you are or how you knew Danny. So thank you for everything, but I've got it from here." I held my non-bloody hand out to him, but he didn't take it. Instead he stared at me as if he was sizing me up, like two warriors across a battlefield, before a grin suddenly split his gorgeous lips and he shook his head in defeat. I felt my heart skip a beat as I realized this was the same man I'd been ogling only a couple of hours earlier and the thoughts of him wearing nothing but that delicious-smelling cologne came flooding back.

"Danny always said you were a feisty one, and I'm glad to see he was right." His bright, blue eyes glinted in the streetlight as he looked toward the children. "Let's let the kids decide, shall we? Jameson and Sarah, do you want to ride on a smelly, old bus to the emergency room for your mom's hand to get taken care of? Or would you rather ride in my car where *maybe* there's a chance we'll stop by the ice cream shop on the way?"

The kids didn't hesitate and before I could open my mouth to say no, they were jumping up and down. "Ice-cream! Yes! Mom, we hate the bus. It smells. Please? He knows Dad!" Their words tumbled over one another and I sighed. Barrett looked at me, his expression softening a bit as he lowered his voice. "The kids could probably use some ice cream, right?"

And I knew what he meant. What they'd witnessed and what they'd been through the past few years hadn't been easy. The next few months probably wouldn't be a joyride, either. If ice cream and a car ride helped them get through what was coming, then it was the least I could do.

I felt another warm and familiar tingle come over me and I sighed, giving in. "Ok, thank you. That is very kind."

He turned to wave at someone in the distance and I saw a luxury Cadillac SUV pull forward and stop in front of us. An older gentleman with gently graying hair at his temples, and a suit which may have rivaled Barrett's, stepped out of the vehicle and opened a side door.

The kids' eyes grew as round as saucers when they saw the interior. Completely blacked-out windows, luxurious leather swivel captain chairs, and a rear seat that could have fit four adults easily, greeted us. Display screens and monitors lined one side of the vehicle with a small, but fully-stocked mini-bar beneath them, and were highlighted by dim under -lighting. It screamed "wealth and luxury" like I'd never in my life dreamed of.

I swallowed, suddenly nervous. "Jameson and Sarah." My voice snapped, full of anxious worry. "Do not, and I repeat, do NOT touch anything."

Nodding, they barely contained their excitement as they clambered over one another, fighting for who got which seat, and I flushed with embarrassment. I was sure both the driver and Barrett were going to scold them for being so rough, but to my surprise Barrett just grinned and opened the door wider.

"Jim, would you mind showing the kids how the monitor works and maybe give them the headphones as well?"

After a few hushed instructions where Jameson quickly got the hang of the console, and both children had Bose noise-canceling head-phones connected to the Bluetooth in the vehicle, I slowly exhaled and climbed in after them.

The kids had turned their captain chairs to the front of the SUV, and were raptly watching a superhero movie on a drop-down screen, now completely oblivious to their surroundings.

I settled into my seat, holding my hand to my chest as the pain I'd forgotten about throbbed in my finger once more.

A heavy presence slid in next to me, the scent of his musky cologne filling my nose, and I stiff-ened. I don't know why I'd assumed he would move to sit in the front with Jim, but I realized suddenly how silly that was. It was his car and driver. Of course, he'd sit in the back.

"Does it hurt?" His voice curled around my ears, the dimness of the vehicle making it sound darker and deeper. A low thrum went through me and I felt my heart do that stupid thing where it sped up for no reason apart from the fact that he was sitting so close to me.

A heavy thigh brushed against mine and suddenly I felt too hot, too flushed. I tried to reason with myself. This was ridiculous. I was only reacting this way because he was ridiculously hot, and I'd been on the receiving end of nothing but asshole behavior from Jason for too long. I honestly couldn't even remember the last time we'd had sex. My vagina probably had sealed itself shut and staked a sign outside the door: "Closed for business."

"It's hurting now. I think the bleeding has mostly stopped." I murmured and inwardly cringed at how breathless and husky it sounded. God, I was pathetic.

The back seat I had thought was so big now seemed too crowded and I tried to scoot away, but he followed me as if my body was a magnet, pulling him toward me.

"May I?" He held his hand out, his eyes searching mine, and try as I might, I couldn't look away. There was something about him. Something both familiar and unknown all at once. I had the distinct feeling that I was standing on a ledge, looking over a cliff, and something was beckoning me forward. All I had to do was take the leap, and I'd fall. Or maybe I'd fly. That warm feeling came over me again, a sense of knowing and peace. But could I trust it?

I gave him my hand, and he bent his head to examine it, carefully peeling back the blood-soaked paper towel with a gentleness that took me by surprise. He seemed so commanding and forceful with Jason, but he held my hand like it was made of glass.

"Hmmm…" He frowned. "It's a deep cut, but I don't think you need stitches. I think I can take care of this." He looked up at me and I gasped, not realizing I'd lowered my head to see what he was looking at. Our faces were mere centimeters from each other. So close that I could see the dark ring of black around his pupils, and the flecks of gray in his iris that showed me they weren't a true aquamarine color. My gaze zeroed-in on his lips and suddenly I felt the chains guarding my vagina drop away, and the sign flip to "Wide open. Especially for a tall, dark and rich guy with the sexiest mouth I've ever seen."

I hissed and scooted back. This was nuts. I

was not attracted to this guy. No matter how familiar he was to me or how much my sex-starved body claimed otherwise.

He frowned, mistaking my hesitance for disbelief. "I promise Leia, I won't hurt you. We can stop at the pharmacy and get the supplies I need. Plus, we need to go there anyway so you can sign for Jameson's medicine."

I blinked, confused by what he was saying. "Jameson's medicine? What do you mean?"

Those sexy fucking lips curled into a smile as he held out a brown bag with the logo of the pharmacy we'd been at earlier. I took it, pulling out the small green bottle of medicine, and my jaw dropped. It was Jameson's medicine. Suddenly, emotion overcame me.

"Why?" My voice shook as I stared at the bottle. "Why are you being so nice to me? Who *are* you?" I looked up, waiting for my answer.

His face was guarded, his eyes holding a shadow to them. Gone was the pleasant smile and kind façade. It was like a mask had fallen away. "I'm not a nice man, Leia." I felt my stomach flutter with anxiousness at his words, wondering what they meant. Did he expect something from me? Had I gone from the frying pan into the fire?

"But I owe Danny a great debt, one I've spent years trying to repay. And if helping you absolve's me of that debt, then I'll gladly pay it."

"What debt? What did he do for you?" Danny had always been kind and generous. It wasn't hard for me to imagine him helping someone out of the goodness of his heart. Sometimes I thought he was almost too good, too kind, too naïve for this world or for the military. I wondered if that's why he'd been taken when he had. The world didn't deserve Danny's.

Barrett's lips pressed into a thin line and he dropped my hand, pulling away from me to settle back into the plush leather of his seat, the darkness of the interior swallowing him whole. "He died."

CHAPTER 5

RHETT

Fucking hell, I was an idiot. I wasn't a nice man. I wasn't even a hero.

As a commander, I'd been a hard-nosed asshole on the best of days. My soldiers had followed every order because I'd led by example and I'd taken care of them, because that's what it means to be a leader. You put yourself last and them first. And they'd obeyed without thought or question. But I would have traded my life for theirs in a heartbeat.

As the CEO of a multi-billion dollar pharmaceutical company, I was down right ruthless. You had to be to survive in a cutthroat business where politicians tried to get their hands in your pockets, and special interest groups tried to tie you to every self-serving project that crossed their minds. Not to mention all the corporate espionage and foreign governments that wanted to steal your intellectual products.

And here I was, sitting next to my dead soldier's widow. A soldier who died because of my orders. And all I was able to think about was how good her sexy fucking mouth would look wrapped around my cock.

With her kids watching a movie two feet away from us.

Guilt stabbed me in the gut, but did nothing to ease the erection I tried to adjust in my pants.

Danny had spoken so much about Leia that it was as if I'd known her before I even met her. We had been friends in the only way that a junior enlisted could be friends with a commanding officer. There had always been a formal line between us. But within those bounds of formality, a friendship sprung up. He understood that being in command meant I made the hard decisions and shouldered the cost. Acting like an asshole and shutting down emotionally was the only way I could get through to the next mission.

The next firefight.

The next death.

He'd seek me out when I had self-isolated from the men with some made up excuse. I'd end up mentoring him on leadership or some other question he'd asked, thinking that I was teaching a junior soldier something about life, but it was Danny who taught me what it meant to truly live for something. He'd lived for Leia and those kids. But he'd died for me.

Because of me.

I watched the shock of my words sink into her. She'd be truly shocked if she knew exactly where my thoughts were a few seconds prior. Where they still were, if I was being honest. I'd thought she was beautiful when I'd seen her in the pharmacy. But to have her sitting less than six inches away from me? Fucking stunning.

Silvery-blonde hair, a porcelain complexion and wide, blue eyes that showed me every expression, every thought that crossed her mind. Did she realize she was blushing while I held her hand? Did she know her eyes darkened and told me she felt the pull of attraction as much as I did? I had to put distance between us before we did something we'd both regret. I'd dropped the bomb of Danny's death, hoping it would be the ice bucket the both of us needed.

Because if she kept looking at my mouth and biting her lip the way she'd been doing, there was no way I was going to not kiss her. My gaze flicked to the front of the vehicle. Just as soon as we were alone. But I didn't want to get *alone*. Did I?

"You're Rhett…"

Her words were so soft I almost didn't catch them, and instinctively leaned my head in closer to hear her, but still kept my gaze focused on a single spot ahead of me. I didn't want meet her gaze. I didn't want to see the accusation and the pain I knew would be there, even if it was what I deserved. I cursed the guilt on my conscious that had forced me to follow her in the first place. I should have left well enough alone.

"Yeah, now you remember." My voice was like a lead weight. Flat and emotionless. It was all business now. She knew who I was and what I did to her husband. There'd be no going back from that. I'd take Leia to the pharmacy, we'd drop off the paperwork, and get her a few bandages for her finger. After that, I would have Jim take her wherever she wanted to go and I would most likely find the first local bar and get blackout drunk. The plan came together, and I almost nodded to myself like a crazy person.

"Danny said that you were the best commander he'd ever served under." Her words were like bullets straight to my heart.

"He also said that you were a prideful, stubborn bastard who would probably blame himself for life for things that were beyond your control."

I whipped my head around to look at her. "When did he tell you that?"

Her smile was soft and there was no sadness, no hatred or anger in her gaze when I met her eyes. Eyes I wanted to drown in. "It was in the letter he wrote to me before his last mission. The one they're supposed to write home in the case of death." Fucking hell, I wasn't prepared for this. It had been two years since I'd separated from the military. Two years since I'd thought about that night and the assault we'd launched to retrieve a high-value target. I hadn't wanted Danny to go. But when I'd assigned his team to a mission that we knew was going to be risky and semi-suicidal at best, he refused to back down.

"Danny was a good man," I growled out, unable to say anything more.

"He was." She sighed, and something in the

sigh made my heart clench. She was looking at her kids. "He was too good. Too kind. Too naïve about the world." A shadow flickered across her face and her gaze found mine again, a fierceness burning in them.

"Sometimes it's ok not to be kind. Because the world does nothing to kindness but kill it. "

I wanted to open my mouth and ask her what the world had done to kill the kindness in her, but before I could speak, we were stopping in front of the pharmacy and Jim was coming around to open our door.

Stepping out on the street, Leia told the kids to wait a moment while Jim stayed with them and that we'd be right back. We entered the drugstore and walked back to where the pharmacy tech was watching us approach with a sense of relief on her face.

Leia spoke to her softly as she signed the slip for the medication and I browsed the aisles looking for the medical supplies I'd need to take care of her cut.

As I finished gathering the last of what I needed and paid for it, Leia approached me.

"I didn't know you owned the entire company!" her voice was whispered shock.

I shrugged. "It wasn't necessary to let you know."

She sputtered, "Well, it was something to that poor tech. She thought she was going to lose her job because of me!"

I shook my head and took hold of her non-injured hand, leading her toward the front door and out onto the street. The streetlights were turning on and I could feel a chill in the evening air. "She wouldn't have lost her job, and she did exactly what I instructed her to do."

She huffed and tugged her hand from me. "Listen, I understand you're feeling some kind of guilt because of Danny and I appreciate you coming to look for me, but I think we should part ways now. The kids don't need ice cream, and I need to find a place to stay for the night and get them settled down for school tomorrow." She held her hand out for the bag of medical supplies. "And I can pay you for that."

There was a stiffness to her now, a subtle pride in the way she held her shoulders and notched her chin up. Somehow, she looked even more stunning than before.

"What do you mean, find a place to stay for

the night?" I growled out as I realized what she was saying, and I didn't like it.

Her eyes narrowed, and she pressed her lips together, refusing to give me an answer. I stepped closer to her, and she tilted her head back to stare up at me. The urge to kiss her overcame me again. What was this magic this woman was casting over me? I couldn't say it was guilt anymore. Guilt didn't send me down a spiral of lust like Leia did. This was something more. I would have said it was fate, but a man like me didn't believe in that shit. But then again, to have run into her in this city, in this pharmacy, on this night. Something about the idea of fate or destiny, it seemed to fit. I could almost see Danny's goofy smile. *"Sometimes life is what it is, Sir. You gotta just go with it or it will go on without you."*

"Tell me you aren't going to a shelter. Tell me you have somewhere to go, or someone to stay with." A rage I didn't understand swirled beneath the surface and I was torn between staying there with Leia or going back to her apartment and beating the shit out of Jason once more.

A guilty look crossed her face and I cursed, turning away from her as I ran a hand through my hair so that I didn't follow through with those thoughts.

"I don't really have a lot of friends here I can call," the meekness in her voice had me turing back toward her, but the look on her face didn't match her tone. "I was going to get a hotel for the night and then I was going to contact the Wild One's Foundation to see what resources they had." Her voice shook but her eyes blazed with a stubborn fire. Leia wouldn't back down without a fight.

"The fuck you are."

She flinched, and I immediately regretted my tone and words, but I continued on. "You'll stay with me. I have an entire house here with rooms I don't use. There's more than enough space for you and the kids. You can stay as long as you need."

She shook her head. "I told you, I won't be a charity case out of some misplaced guilt you have, Rhett." The sound of my name on her tongue unleashed a spiral of desire, but it was the way she stood her ground that had me in a chokehold. She might have been broken by life, but the fierceness Danny spoke of was still there, lurking under the surface. A sleeping lioness waiting to wake up.

"Let's get something straight here, little lioness. I don't do charity cases. Now," I opened the Cadillac's door, and the kids turned toward us, eyes wide and curious as they were obviously watching us talk from inside the SUV. "What kind of ice cream do you like?"

Their eyes darted back and forth between us as she continued to glaring at me, indecision clearly written all over her face. Finally, she sighed and her shoulders slumped in defeat. I hated seeing it. I didn't want her to think I was pushing her to do something she didn't want. I wanted her to see that she could trust me. That I had her best interests in mind. That I could be a strength for her to rest in, not run from. I didn't know how I would prove it, but I was determined now that this was going to be my goal for as long as she was staying with me. As of this moment, Leia Morrow was my sole mission. And I would not fail.

Once again, I could almost see Danny smile.

CHAPTER 6

LEIA

I wanted to refuse him.

I wanted to tell Jameson and Sarah to get out of the car and storm off toward the nearest bus stop with my head held high and my pride intact. But with one look at my children, I knew I couldn't do that. For all that Danny had talked about him and raved about him, Rhett was a stranger to me. And I was more than aware of all the risks I was taking by even getting into his car, but something deep inside me whispered that I could trust him if I would let myself. And what had he done but helped since the moment he showed up at my door?

I sighed in defeat, but in reality, I was relieved. The idea of spending the next few nights in a rundown hotel hadn't appealed to me, and something told me that Jason wouldn't just let us go without a fight. He'd be looking all over town for me and had probably already put a block on my cards to force me back to him. Staying at Rhett's for the night would offer some protection until I was able to get in contact with people who could help us.

Rhett leaned in to say something to the kids and Mr. Jim while I was lost in thought, then suddenly I realized he was speaking to me again.

"What do you say, Leia, is that ok?"

I blinked, "I'm sorry, is what ok?

Mr. Jim looked at me and smiled. "I was telling Mr. Barrett that the cook has recently stocked the fridge at the house with all sorts of ice cream goodies and I thought that since it was getting late, the children might like to have dinner and then dessert?"

"Oh!" Crap, I'd forgotten about the dinner I'd been making before everything had fallen apart. "I'm so sorry, you're right. I completely forgot about dinner." I winced as I instinctively wrung my hands in nervousness. How could I have been so stupid?

Rhett grabbed my hand and pulled me into the vehicle behind him, and even when he settled back into the seat, didn't let it go. His thumb tracing against my skin sent little sparks of electricity through me.

"There was no need to apologize, Leia, you've been through a lot. Dinner is the last thing you need to worry about right now." His thumb continued to graze my skin and this time, as he held onto my hand, I let him. There was a comfort and strength in that simple gesture that, for a while, I wanted to cling to.

The ride to his house wasn't long, and we fell into a comfortable silence with my hand still held in his. I wasn't really sure if he even realized he was still holding onto it, but I wasn't going to break the spell.

We pulled into a gated community and I stared, wide-eyed, out the window of his car as we drove past homes that were easily the size of my apartment building, plus some.

"Woah, Mom, are these castles?" Sarah's awed voice filled the quiet cabin space, and I heard Rhett chuckle.

"Hardly. Have ever seen a castle?"

She shook her head, blonde curls bouncing. "No, we were supposed to go to Disney World and see the princess's castle with Papa Jason." Her eyes grew dark. "But then he never took us. He never took us a lot of places." My heart shattered. How many promises had Jason made to us that he'd broken? How many times had I *let* him break them? All because I'd been so afraid of what life was going to be like after Danny's death. All because I'd been afraid to truly live.

A dark look passed over Rhett's handsome face, but he said nothing more as we were pulling into a wide, circular driveway before a modern looking tri-level home. It was nearly solid black and made of steel and concrete as opposed to the rest of the neighborhood that featured more classic looking designs and stone fronts.

The vehicle came to a stop in front of obsidian colored double doors, and bright lights flooded the walkway. I could see at least a dozen security cameras and even more motion sensors throughout the rest of the clean and simplistic landscaping. I raised a brow as we approached the door. "You certainly have a nice security set up. Someone might think you were overcompensating for something." Maybe it was the fact that my hand still tingled from where his thumb had left goosebumps on my skin. Or maybe it was that I'd been enveloped in the spicy scent of his cologne for the past half hour, but I couldn't keep the teasing innuendo out of my voice. Immediately, I cringed. How long had it been since I'd actually flirted with someone? Did I even remember how? Now that I was single again, did I even want to think about the possibility of dating again? Or even having sex?

My gaze zeroed in on his lips as a devilish smirk curled at the corner of his lips. I felt my stomach do flips as his eyes darkened and he leaned toward me, his lips barely brushing against my ear while he scanned his thumb into a keypad hidden near the door. "I promise you, little lioness, I don't need to overcompensate for anything. And the security is precautionary." I hissed in a breath at the way his voice sent vibrations down to my very core. "I protect what's mine."

Okay yes, my body was telling me that sex was very much still on the menu for me.

Then the door opened and the kids, who had been oohing and ahhing over the glimpses of a pool they'd spotted from the driveway, went running through the front doors with all the energy of two stampeding elephants.

An older woman with gently graying hair and

an apron tied around her waist stood ready to greet us, and she smiled from ear to ear as I tried to grab the kids' attention before they could knock over anything that was valuable.

"Hello dear. You must be Leia, and this is Jameson and Sarah?" Her gray eyes sparkled with warmth and I couldn't help but smile back. "I'm Pam, the housekeeper and cook. You've already met my husband, Jim."

"Hello Pam," I reached a hand out to shake hers and her eyes went wide at the sight of the bloody paper towel still wrapped around my fingers. "Oh dear, yes, we need to get that taken care of right away!" She murmured in alarm. I'd been so distracted by everything that I'd all but forgotten about the dull throbbing, and blushed in embarrassment.

Rhett held up the bag of supplies he purchased and leaned in to give Pam a quick kiss on her cheek. "Already on it, Pammy. Can you take the kids into the kitchen if dinner is ready? I promised them ice cream." He lowered his voice to a conspirators whisper, and Pam nodded with another concerned glance down at my hand before calling the kids to follow her. The familiar way he greeted her took me by surprise, but then he was guiding me down the hall toward a guest powder room just off the main living area where he flicked the lights on before closing the door behind us.

"You ready?"

I was too distracted by the gorgeous bathroom with its floor-to-ceiling black marble and gold accents to notice how close he was standing, but when I turned around, there he was. And despite the size of the space and the twelve-foot ceiling, it was like his presence filled the room. He'd removed his suit jacket, laying it across the wide counter and I gulped nervously as he rolled his white shirt sleeves up revealing thick, muscular forearms. My eyes drifted from his sleeves to his neck where he'd loosened his tie and I could see the peek of solid muscle beneath the shirt that strained against the fabric.

I started to back away but was met with the cool, marble counter against my back, as he carefully opened up the pharmacy bag and began laying supplies out.

"You don't have to do this..." My voice was soft, strained, and maybe he mistook how it shook for nervousness because he flicked a glance in my direction, one brow arching over those gorgeous eyes, and smiled.

"Don't worry, Leia, I've got you." He patted the counter. "Come here." The command was innocent. He only wanted me to come closer, right? But the way it reverberated down my back and curled around the base of my spine had me practically in a puddle. My feet moved a few inches towards him, but I still stood mostly in the same place. He frowned and before I knew it, had hauled me closer to him, picking me up as if I weighed nothing more than a feather, to place me on the counter. I gasped.

"What are you doing?"

He moved in between my thighs and reached across me to turn the water on in the sink. "You were thinking about kicking me out to take care of this yourself." I started to shake my head in denial, but then he stopped me with a pointed look. "I could see it in your eyes." He looked back down, carefully peeling away the blood-soaked paper towel bit by bit, so that it didn't pull open the wound again. "I don't know why, Leia, I can't really explain it, and I've been trying to reason with myself for the last hour now. But I need to do this for you." His voice was low, a burning whisper of emotion in the dark timbre. "You've been taking care of everyone but yourself for so long. I knew you wouldn't let me unless I forced it." The remaining paper towel was gently peeled away completely now, and he held my hand between us, the smell of dried blood and anti-septic ointment mixing with his cologne.

He brought his eyes back to mine. "Please?"

The question shook me.

The weight of it.

Innocent and yet not.

I nodded and licked my lips nervously. His eyes zeroed-in on my mouth and he looked away with a frown, furring his eyebrows as he held my hand under the water and washed away the blood. He was right. I had been about to insist that I could take care of the cut and bandage everything myself. That's what I'd always done. Not only with Jason, but with Danny as well. I'd taken care of everything. The house, the bills, the children, our life. Danny would have sat next to me and supported me. But he would never have thought of every little detail, scrutinizing every inch of my hand and meticulously cleaning away any evidence of blood. And Jason? He'd have let me drive myself to the ER without even a thought, and he would have only checked on me once he realized I'd been gone too long.

I bit down on my lip to hold back a slight hiss of pain as Rhett had to pinch the edges of the wound together slightly in order to line up the butterfly bandages. His eyes flicked to my lips, and he groaned. "Don't do that Leia."

I blinked, startled. "What do you mean?"

He didn't look at me as he began wrapping my hand in soft, white gauze. "It's taking all of my self control not to do the things I've been thinking about since I saw you in the pharmacy earlier, little lioness. I meant what I said. I'm not a nice man and you are a temptation that is testing every bit of my restraint."

He finished tucking the edges of the bandage but didn't let my hand go, and I was suddenly very aware of how my legs were spread, his hips between them and his body pressing against my thighs. My entire body flushed with heat as I leaned back and looked up at him. I'd never had a man talk to me like this and look at me like he meant every word. That feeling of standing on a ledge, waiting to fall or fly, came over me again. Maybe it was the emotional roller-coaster of the day, or maybe it was the fact that every inch of my body was yearning to be touched in a way I'd never experienced before, but the next words out of my mouth weren't words I'd ever imagined saying to a man, ever. But the minute they were out of my mouth, they felt right.

"So do them."

CHAPTER 7

RHETT

Blood rushed from my head to my balls so fast I became dizzy.

I'd picked her up to place her on the counter in an attempt to cage her in and prevent her from leaving. I hadn't planned on her spreading her legs, drawing me in between her sweet thighs and staring up at me, her eyes burning with heat and desire.

Desire that matched my own.

I watched as a soft, pink blush spread over her pretty skin, my eyes tracing the path from her neck to her cheeks.

I must have taken too long to respond, because she frowned and looked away. "I'm sorry, I shouldn't have said that."

The hesitancy, the guarded look was back in her eyes. I grabbed her chin and forced her to look at me.

"Stop. Don't apologize ever again, Leia. I'm the one who let my cock run away with my mouth." At the word "cock", her eyes dilated and she licked her lips. Did she like that?

"Tell me what you want." I stared into her eyes, praying she gave me the answer I wanted, but resigning myself to whatever she said next. If she told me to fuck off, I'd gladly do it. In the shower. With my hand. Thinking of her on her knees, her pretty pink tongue out and wait—

"You." Her voice was soft, but firm. There was no hesitancy in it.

"I want you." My dick swelled at the words. "And I want to forget, and I want to remember at the same time."

I frowned. Was she looking for a rebound? A way to ease the pain from the trauma of the past several years? I would provide it. There was no way I could tell her no at this point. But I wasn't so sure I could handle being just a one-night stand for her, either. "What is it you want to remember?" My thumb softly traced the full curve of her bottom lip.

"What it's like to live." Her words cut through me.

I knew what she meant. Probably more than she would ever realize. Hadn't I been living as a shell of a man for the past several years? Life after the military had been nothing but meetings, takeovers, mergers and money. I'd thought I'd be able to appease the growing darkness in me by waging war on my competition, much like I'd waged war on the battlefield. But the ghosts of my past were never silenced, and all they did was drain me until I was as dry as the desert inside. Colorless. Bland. Until her.

I pulled away and I could see the disappointment creep into her gaze as she mistook my silence for hesitancy. I shook my head. "This isn't a rejection, little lioness. I'm going to give you exactly what you want, but it's not going to be right now."

Her lips turned down in a soft pout as she frowned in confusion. "What do you mean?"

I couldn't resist and I edged closer to her again, my hands gripping her thighs as I pulled her into my hips, letting her feel just how hard she had me. I nipped her bottom lip, and she opened her mouth, but I didn't kiss her.

"Make no mistake, Leia. I'm going to fuck you. I'm going to give you everything that prick never could. I'm going to not only make you forget he even has a name, but I'm going to make you feel so alive and so good when you're coming on my tongue, my hands, my cock, that you'll think you'd never truly lived before me."

She gasped, her mouth a wide "O" of shock, and I watched as the pretty pink flush to her skin traveled from her cheeks to her neck, down to where I could just see it disappear over the tops of her breasts. I couldn't wait to find out if that blush continued over her whole body and what she would look like all pink from the marks I'd leave on her skin.

Because there was no doubt about it. I was going to mark her.

She might only want me for one night. But I'd use this one night to make her mine.

I stepped away and left her staring after me as she tried to process the words I said. She didn't understand yet what she'd asked of me, but I did. Leia wanted to feel what it was like to live again? Then I was going to show her.

I wasn't a pretty boy with pretty words. I took what I wanted and destroyed any competition that stood in my way. My tastes weren't for the soft or the weak and there would be no time for expensive dinners or fancy gifts. But my little lioness wasn't weak. She would get all of me. The dark parts of me. The broken and the bitter. And I would give her exactly what she wanted in return. And if she rejected me after? So be it. But Leia would know what it meant to live.

And maybe, for just a night, I'd know it too.

I opened the door and stepped aside, watching as she slipped down off the counter and eyed me curiously.

"Let's eat. Pam makes a mean steak sandwich."

At the mention of food, I heard her stomach rumble, but she gasped. "Oh, my gosh. The kids. I need to get them settled and ready for school tomorrow. And I need to get Jameson his medicine."

I stopped her as she rushed out the door and hauled her back against me, my mouth finding hers. Her response was instantaneous as she melted against me, her sweet lips parting under mine as I devoured her. Inhaled her. Fuck, she was perfect. She tasted like the sweetest dessert I'd ever had and I wanted to do nothing more than lock the bathroom door and forget every word I'd just said to her as I bent her over the bathroom counter and watched her orgasm in the mirror.

But that wasn't what she asked of me. I pulled back and looked down at her. "Stop worrying, Leia. The kids are fine. Pam and Jim have it under control and I'll make sure Jameson has his medicine and that you say goodnight when the kids are settled. But you need to relax. You've been putting everyone else before yourself so much so that you feel guilty even taking the time to get a wound taken care of."

She frowned and moved away from me, putting some distance between us. "Rhett, I know you're just trying to help and I will not deny that I am *very*," she cleared her throat and blushed deeper. "... appreciative of your efforts. But these are my kids. And they've been through hell." I could see the pain in her eyes and the thought that she refused to voice. That she'd been the one to put them through that hell. "I need to be there for them and to show them it's going to be ok."

I nodded. "Ok, let's go take care of the kids then."

She blinked and gave me a confused look.

"What do you mean 'let's go take care of the kids'?"

I grabbed my suit jacket off the counter and stepped out into the hallway, making my way to the back of the house and into the kitchen.

"Well, you said that you need to make sure they're settled and ready for school tomorrow and you don't feel comfortable letting someone else do it, so we'll do it together."

I could hear her hurrying after me, but I didn't pause until I felt her hand on my arm and she jerked on it, bringing me to a stop, forcing me to look down at her again. She was so tiny, barely reaching the middle of my chest. "Why?" Was all she asked, her eyes searching mine, questioning me. *Questioning my motives.* I could have smiled and given her some answer about just wanting to help. But I knew that wasn't what she needed. Leia needed the truth, even if the truth hurt.

"Because you've been doing this by yourself long enough. And I'm not talking about just with dipshit. I'm talking about with Danny too. You did it all Leia. Even a lion can't hunt alone and you've been on your own for too long. In more ways than one." I grabbed her chin and tipped her head up, my thumb running across her sexy bottom lip as the urge to kiss her came over me again. "You think you're weak because you need help, *right now*. But you've never been the weak one. They were."

I dropped my hand and continued on the path to the kitchen where the children were finishing up their ice cream, and an animated discussion with Pam and Jim. Leia said nothing, not even to defend Danny, and instead swept past me to herd the children out of the kitchen and toward the upstairs bedrooms. I followed and didn't wait for her to tell me what she needed. By the time she'd inspected their bedrooms and found the bathroom, I'd already had towels, toothbrushes and other items ready to go. While it had been awhile since I'd been around kids, I wasn't a stranger to them and had been involved in helping my brother with his kids for a time.

I helped her walk Jameson and Sarah through their bedtime routine, listening to her whisper soft reassurances to them as she tucked them into their beds, then I said good night with promises that they could swim in the heated pool tomorrow after school. I thought she might argue with me over it and say something absurd like they wouldn't be here in the evening, but all she did was give me a long look and then kissed the children one last time before shutting off the lights and following me out to the hall.

I walked her to her bedroom and watched with growing anticipation as she fidgeted nervously, her eyes flicking back and forth from the door to me. I could tell she wanted to talk about what I'd said earlier, but I didn't want to give her the chance to back out.

Leaning in, I braced my hands on the doorframe as she pressed her back against the dark wood.

"Pick a safe word."

She blinked. "A what?"

"You heard me, little lioness. Pick a safe word." I cocked my head slightly. "Or have you changed your mind?"

She shook her head slowly, her tongue nervously darting out to wet her lips. "I meant what I said. I want you." She cocked her head and I could see that same boldness and fire flicker through her eyes again. "And I know you want me too."

"Then pick a safe word, Leia. Because I plan to do exactly what you've asked me to do. I'm going to push you to the very brink of what you can handle. And I'm going to do it over and over and over again." I leaned down, running my nose against the soft skin of her neck to the tender spot just below her ear. Breathing her in until her scent was buried deep within my lungs. "Unless you don't think you can handle it?"

"Muffin!" she blurted out, and I pulled away to look down at her, arching a brow at her outburst.

"My safe word is muffin." I grinned. She didn't know it, but she'd just sealed her fate.

I stepped away from her. "Good girl." And then I left her standing at her door.

"Wait! When am I supposed to be ready to use it?" I could hear the confusion and disbelief in her voice, but I didn't turn around to look at her.

"When you least expect it."

CHAPTER 8

LEIA

What the fuck was I thinking? A *safe word?* I wasn't sure who I was more upset with, myself, or the arrogant sex on legs that had just walked away when I was practically begging him to fall into bed with me.

I had never used a safe word before. Not that it was something I was unfamiliar with. I'd read my share of smutty romances and knew exactly what he meant when he'd asked me for one.

I could have said no right then. I could have told him I wasn't interested in that kind of thing and we could have just gone our separate ways. A little embarrassed but dignity fully intact. But had I? No. Instead, I'd opened up my mouth and blurted out the first word that popped into my brain. Muffin.

The way his eyes had darkened when he'd leaned into me, and the smirk that curled up the corner of his lips had left me practically dripping. I don't know that I could have even given a different answer. All I knew was that the dark promises behind his words had me dying to know if he could fulfill them. And somehow, I knew he could.

I moved into the room he'd shown me to and gasped.

It was gorgeous. I wasn't sure that he hadn't given me the master suite instead of a guest room like he'd given the kids.

The walls were a dark burgundy color that contrasted with the light wood floors. It gave off both a modern and decadent feel. The bed was king-size and layered in plush, cream blankets and so many pillows I could have drowned in them. It wasn't until I was looking around the room admiring it, that I realized I had absolutely nothing with me. Not a single thing to my name at all.

I groaned. I would have to go back to my apartment to get my belongings, although I doubted Jason would be agreeable to just boxing them up for me. At the thought, I pulled my phone out of my purse and checked the notifications. I'd silenced it once I'd left the apartment, knowing that he'd be calling and texting me non-stop until I answered.

Sure enough, there were at least a dozen missed calls and double the amount of messages. I scrolled through them until the last one and a chill went through me when I read the text.

> Jason: You think you can run from me, Leia? You belong to me.

> You can't survive without me.

> There's nowhere you can go that I can't find you.

> I always know where you are.

> You have one chance to come back and then I will come for you.

> And you don't want to find out what will happen after that.

It wasn't the first time Jason had said something like that to me. Usually followed up with an "I'm just kidding! Baby, it was a joke." When I'd tell him how creepy that was. I wondered for a moment if he really knew where I was at, but then dismissed the thought. There was no way he'd have any clue where Rhett lived and even if he did, the security system here would surely alert us to an intruder.

The message distracted me enough that I almost missed the tray sitting next to the bed, but as I stood up to find the bathroom and shower, I saw it glinting in the dim light. Lifting the lid, I smiled. There was a wrapped sandwich and drink waiting for me. Rhett's words about always putting myself last echoed through my mind, and I realized I had been so focused on getting the kids settled that I'd forgotten to eat. But he'd remembered.

My heart skipped a beat with an emotion I didn't want to acknowledge. What he'd said about Danny and Jason had been true. It's why when I'd started to defend Danny, I couldn't. Because he was right. Both men were as different as night and day. And yet both had, in their own way, never lifted a finger to help me when I needed it. Danny would have stood by and waited until I told him what I wanted him to do. Jason would have just scoffed at me and said it was my job, not his. I'd always done everything on my own. But tonight

Rhett had been there without me saying a word. He'd just seen what needed to be done and did it. And despite his insistence that he wasn't a nice man. I scoffed and shook my head.

I couldn't let a couple of nice gestures and helpful hands turn my head and convince me he was the Prince Charming of this story. Hadn't I learned the hard way that there was no Prince Charming? There weren't any fairy godmothers or coaches turning into pumpkins at midnight. There was only my heart, and it had already been broken enough. I wasn't sure I could even put the cracks of it back together anymore. Grief had shattered it like it was made of glass. And in the brokenness of trying to heal, I'd allowed someone to come in and destroy it even more.

But no more. I was going to take what he offered me; food, shelter, his dark promises of mind-blowing pleasure— and not look back. I meant what I said. I wanted to live again, but I wanted to live my story. Not someone else's.

A piece of paper fluttered to the ground, and I picked it up, sucking in a breath as I saw what was on it. Maybe not such a Prince Charming after all. Before me was a checklist, and suddenly the reality of my chosen safe word sank into me. I picked up the pen that was left on the table with the tray and before I could talk myself out of it, quickly checked off yes's and no's then folded it up and placed it back on the tray. There was no going back now.

Inhaling the sandwich, I made my way to the ensuite bathroom, once again my jaw dropping in shock. Was I in a house or a spa? I decided no matter what, even if this spell had to break at midnight, I would not look the kinky fairy godfather in the mouth. I would just file this away as a dream and something I would work to provide for my children someday. Manifest that shit until one day it was a reality. Something I used to do when I was young and just starting out as a new associate in my marketing firm. Only then it had been all about white picket fences and maybe a golden doodle for the family. But now I knew I wanted more. More than what I had before. More than what I'd dreamed of. And it would start after I took full advantage of the multiple shower heads in the floor-to-ceiling marble tiled shower. I found a guest robe hanging up and toiletries in the drawers and as I undressed; I took a long look at myself in the mirror. And for the first time in years, I saw in my reflection a glimpse of the woman I'd once been. For the first time in a long time, I saw hope.

Rhett's blue eyes glinted in the darkness, his hot breath trailing a path from my knee up my thigh until his lips were hovering just above my pussy. I writhed beneath him, wanting to reach down and urge him to put his mouth where he'd taunted and promised me he would. I couldn't reach him, though. Frustration flared through me. This was my sex dream, so why couldn't I do what I wanted? I'd crawled in between the silken sheets of Rhett's bed, waiting for him to come. But then I'd fallen asleep and had dreamt of him instead. In my dream, his firm hands had stroked and massaged me from my calves to my thighs, gently pulling the sheet away from my skin in a silken caress.

His lips and teeth had nipped my breasts, sucking my nipples into his mouth as he groaned. "So fucking perfect. Look at you, Leia. Even asleep, you respond to me. I've been dying, waiting to taste that sweet pussy. How wet are you for me?"

I moaned. "So wet, please, Rhett."

He chuckled, a dark sound that had me shivering beneath him as he moved down my body. "Please what, my little lioness? Tell me what you want."

"Eat me, fuck me, make me come!" I rolled my hips against him, urging him on.

"Your wish is my command." At the first touch of his tongue on my clit, my eyes flew open.

Oh fuck, it wasn't a dream.

And I couldn't move.

My arms were pulled above my head and secured in soft restraints. My legs were spread with similar restraints at the ankles and Rhett was there between my legs with a devilish look in his eye as he sucked my clit into his mouth and I bucked against him. All around us, red candles flickered in the darkness, casting shadows that danced over our skin.

"What are you doing?" I gasped and tugged at the restraints.

He paused long enough to pierce me with a serious look. "You read the list, correct?" Oh shit. The list I'd checked off earlier. I nodded, flushed and torn between wanting him back between my legs and unsure about where this was going. How had he gotten me restrained while I slept? Or had moved around the room lighting candles, for that matter? The thought should have frightened me, but all it did was send pulses of desire through me.

"Your safe word is the key. Do you want to use it?" He cocked his head, waiting for my answer, but his fingers were tracing lazy patterns through the slick heat at my core.

Did I? Our eyes locked, and I knew the answer.

I shook my head.

No.

I didn't want to use it.

I'd asked him to make me feel what it was to live again, and he was doing just that. I'd never felt more alive than in this moment right now. Unable to take control. Completely exposed. Completely vulnerable. Completely at his mercy.

"Good girl."

And then his mouth was on me again. Licking, teasing, sucking. He didn't just eat my pussy; he *devoured* me. My entire body felt like it was going to come off the bed as the orgasm ripped through me. If it wasn't for the restraints, it might have.

"Did you just come for me?" His voice was a

dark whisper against my ear. When had he moved? I nodded.

"Words, Leia." The command was followed by a light smack directly over my sensitive clit, and I groaned.

"Yes, I did."

"Good. That's one. The next time you will tell me when you're coming. Do you understand?"

I opened my eyes and searched for him in the dim light. "This is just a one-time thing, Rhett."

Was I sex drunk? I'd just had the best orgasm of my life only from his mouth and he was telling me there was going to be a next time? God, if I didn't want there to be. But I had to establish the boundaries now. I may have been restrained, but I was still in control.

He looked at me, a dark brow arching in question. "I wasn't referring to tonight. I was talking about the number of orgasms I'm going to give you."

My mouth fell open. "Oh..."

"I told you earlier. I'm going to make you come over and over and over again until you forget your own name. I'm going to give you exactly what you asked me for, even if it's just for one night." His fingers plunged into my opening, filling and stretching me, and I moaned.

"Now, remember to tell me when you're coming..." Then his tongue followed his fingers, and I was lost once more in indescribable bliss.

CHAPTER 9

RHETT

She tasted like golden honey.

Like I was drinking the nectar of the gods and I wouldn't be able to get enough.

I'd never get enough.

Leia was an addiction, and there was no cure.

This was the last thing I'd planned for during my time in Wild. But it was right where I needed to be. When I'd slipped into her room, she'd been sleeping like an angel. Her silvery-blonde hair fanned out across the pillow like a halo. I knew she wouldn't wake as I moved around the room. I knew how to move without a whisper of a sound, and it was nothing for me to set everything up for what I had planned.

I was starving, and Leia was about to be my

feast. She moaned softly, her lips parting in her sleep as I'd pulled first one arm and then the other above her head, securing them. Then repeated the process with her legs. The straps had already been there, just waiting for a moment like this. A delicacy that I rarely indulged in, and when I did, it was hard to find a woman who fit my tastes so specifically. A woman like Leia. When I'd scanned the checklist and saw she'd checked yes to restraints, I knew there was no going back.

I'd give her every opportunity to tell me no. To use her safe word. *Muffin.* I'd chuckled and she stirred in her sleep, a frown marring her perfect skin. It had to have been the cutest, most non-safe-word-sounding word, ever. A contradiction just like she was. Soft and delicate. But underneath was pure steel.

Then she'd woken up, a lioness ready to claw and fight her way free, until I'd given her the key and she realized she was in control all along. I couldn't remember a time when I'd been more nervous, afraid that she would reject me and use her word. To be honest, there was a dark part of me that wasn't sure I could let her go. But then she'd shaken her head no, and I'd devoured her like the starving man I was.

Did she know how desperate she made me? Darkness crept in the edges of my vision and I knew it was going to be hard to hold back the urge I had to mark her, claim her, and make her mine in every way.

She writhed beneath me, her pussy fluttering around my fingers as I pulled another orgasm from her. This time she tipped her head back and screamed, "Oh God, I'm coming!" I smiled. She was obedient. Just like I knew she would be.

"Good, baby girl. That was two." She was panting, her eyes closed, her entire body flushed a deep pink, and I gripped her hips, my fingers digging into the delicate skin hard enough that I knew there would be imprints in the morning.

"Ready to give me more?" Her eyes flew open wide.

"More?" she breathed, sounding incredulous.

"Yes, more. Don't tell me you've never had multiple orgasms before?" Her cheeks blushed a deeper pink and a sudden possessiveness came over me.

"I'm... I'm not sure..."

The snarl that came out of my mouth surprised me. Holy fuck, I wasn't going to last. I was going to be the first to show her just how much pleasure her body could handle. And I wanted to be the last as well. I was going to own every kiss, every moan, every orgasm.

Leia might not be mine, but fuck me if I wasn't already completely and devastatingly hers. I reached up without hesitation and unsnapped the restraints on her hands, then made quick work of releasing her legs.

She looked at me, confused for a moment, but then I pinned her to the bed with my body, my cock pressing against her opening.

"I wanted to take my time with you. I wanted to draw out your pleasure for hours. To make you come repeatedly until you begged me to stop. But I can't wait anymore and your first time with multiples can be overwhelming." I explained while I cupped her cheeks, forcing her to look at me. I pressed into her and paused.

"I'm going to fuck you now, Leia. I'm going to wreck this pretty pussy. Is that what you want?"

"Yes. Holy fuck, yes, that's what I want, Rhett."

"Good girl." I slid inside in one stroke. Her pussy gripped my cock like a vice, tight, wet, and perfect in every way.

She moaned and I could feel her legs and hips

spreading as she adjusted to my size. But I didn't give her any more time before I was rocking into her, driving my hips into hers as I gripped her legs and pinned them further back so that I could reach a deeper angle.

She took me, all of me, and then surprised me when she gripped her own legs, spreading them wider.

"Yes baby, that's it. Spread your legs for me, hold them open so I can fuck you."

At my words, I saw her eyes roll back and flutter, her body tensing as I sensed her nearing another orgasm. So my little lioness liked dirty talk? Well, then I'd give it to her. I sat back and gripped her hair, pulling her forward, forcing her eyes open so she could see where our bodies were joined.

"Watch, Leia. See how good your pussy takes my cock? Like it was meant for it." Her eyes were glazed over and transfixed as she watched me slam, hard and deep, inside her tight walls.

"I want to fill this pussy. I want to come so deep inside you that you'll never get me out." She moaned, and I released her hair, bending over her to pull a taut nipple into my mouth. "Is that where you want me, baby? Inside of you?"

She nodded, and I bit down slightly on her nipple. "Words, Leia." I reprimanded. "Tell me where you want me to come."

"Oh god, fill me up Rhett, come inside me. Please!" The last word was a scream as I drove into her hard.

Need took over, and all I could do was drive my hips into hers over and over again.

"Come with me, Leia. Come on my cock while I use your pussy."

She exploded then, her entire body shaking as she gushed around me. Her words were lost as my own orgasm drove me deep inside her. Filling her. Marking her. Making her mine.

My heartbeat was in my ears as I collapsed, pulling her to me.

She murmured against my chest, her words muffled, and I pulled away slightly so I could hear her.

"Are you ok?"

"That...was...wow."

I chuckled and placed a kiss on the top of her head. "Glad I could deliver."

She pulled away from me, her eyes searching mine. "I wasn't sure what to expect. I've never done anything like that before."

I nodded. "I know. Thank you for trusting me."

Her teeth worried her bottom lip, and I had to fight the urge to kiss her again. "I don't know why I trusted you. I mean, obviously, I wanted... things..." She blushed and I couldn't resist teasing her.

"Things? You mean you wanted me to fuck you?" She blushed again, but her eyes danced.

"Yes, Rhett, I wanted *that.*"

I smirked. "So say it. Say, 'I wanted to fuck you, Rhett'."

She rolled her eyes

"I wanted to fuck you, Rhett."

Hearing those dirty words out of her mouth had me hard again.

"Careful, little lioness. Keep talking like that and I'll break my promise to take it slow."

I felt her tense and then shift away. Unease stirred in my gut. I didn't like the guarded look that was on her face now.

"Rhett, listen. That was just amazing, mind-blowing, even..." I gave her a cocky grin. "But this really is a one-time thing. I appreciate all you've done to help and what you've said, but..."

I cut her off with a kiss, not wanting to hear what she was going to say next.

"It's not a one time thing, Leia, it's a *one-night* thing. And there is still a lot of night left. I told you I was going to push you to your limits, and I meant it." I growled against her lips.

Her lips were swollen and pouty by the time I was done tasting every corner of her mouth. She pulled away, "But you said multiples could be overwhelming for me...."

I nodded and stood up, moving to a large, leather Chesterfield chair near the window where I sat down, spreading my legs and palming my erection in my hand. Leia's eyes tracked every movement from where she sat on her knees in the middle of the bed. "They can be when they're back to back like that. But I'm going to draw them out slower now. Tease and bring you right to the edge until you think you can't handle anymore, and then do it all over again." I stroked my cock, her eyes following my hand, and she licked her lips. "And... I never said anything about multiples being overwhelming for *me.*"

"Oh.." She breathed, her eyes transfixed on my hand as I slowly stroked my cock, taking some of the pre-cum from the tip and spreading it around the head. She licked her lips, and I squeezed the tip harder.

"Do you enjoy watching?"

She nodded, and I stopped. "Use your words." She shifted nervously and blushed. "If you want to continue to watch me, then you need to tell me what you like. Don't be a coward."

Her eyes flashed at my challenge. "I like watching you stroke yourself."

"Good girl." I praised and resumed leisurely stroking myself. "Play with yourself while you watch me." She licked her lips again and spread her legs wider, her fingers finding their way to her center, where she stroked her clit and moaned.

"Look at you, little lioness. Such a needy little thing. Are your fingers enough? Do you need more?" She quivered on the bed, her fingers plunging into her pussy repeatedly in time to the movements of my hand on my hard length.

"More..." she moaned. "I need more."

I stopped stroking and sat back. "Then come take it."

She rose from the bed like a goddess rising from the sea, her sexy hips swaying as she walked toward me. There was need and fire burning in her pale blue eyes, as she placed first one leg and then the other over my thighs.

"What is it you need, Rhett?" Her husky voice curled around me as she stayed poised over my cock, her wetness gliding over the tip. My fingers dug into the arms of the chair as I resisted the urge to thrust upward into her. Leia was in control now.

I stared into her eyes, drowning in them, and answered honestly."You Leia. I need you."

She smirked, leaning forward to brush her lips against mine as she sank down onto me. "Then take me," she whispered.

I lost control. Grabbing her hips, I raised her up to slam her back down on my cock. Over and over bouncing her on me as need and a darker urge drove me.

The last thought I remembered as I stood up with her and walked us back to the bed where I withdrew before throwing her down onto her stomach, lining up my cock and driving into her again, was that I didn't care if she only wanted this to be one night. Leia Morrow was mine. And I wasn't going to give her up.

CHAPTER 10

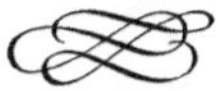

LEIA

Softness enveloped me. I snuggled down into the blankets and pillows, practically purring in contentment. My body felt deliciously sore and languid at the same time. Memories of the night came flooding back.

Rhett.

The way he'd commanded my body like he was waging war on it. Pulling one orgasm after another from me. He'd done exactly what he'd promised, bringing me just to the edge before he'd back off and switch to something new. Teasing every sense and nerve ending until I was a sobbing mess.

And then when I'd finally been allowed to scream my release, his name had been the only word I could say. Over and over again. Just like he'd told me I would.

Only then had he stopped, coming with me and filling me so deeply it felt like he'd marked my very soul.

The thought sobered me. One night of amazing sex meant nothing. I couldn't afford to think in terms of soul or anything else. I had to plan and prepare for the future and my children's future.

I checked the time on my phone and realized I only had a few minutes before I needed to get the kids dressed and out the door to school. Panic hit me and I flung the covers off the bed as my feet hit the floor and I scrambled to find my clothes. What had happened to my alarm? Why didn't it go off?

I pulled one shoe on and then another as I hopped down the hall. "Jameson! Sarah! You need to wake up! We're going to be late for school!"

I burst into their room, but it was empty. Fear gripped me. Their beds were neatly made as if they'd never even slept in them. Their back packs were gone.

I whipped around, heading back into the

hallway and ran blindly into a muscular chest. A bare chest. A sexy bare chest that dipped down into six-pack abs and a narrowed waist where a set of gray sweatpants hung off his hips, like they were questioning their decision to stay put.

I gasped, "Oh my God, Rhett, I'm so sorry. The kids, do you know where they are?"

He cocked his head, a smile flicking the corner of his lips up. "Do you always barrel around the house like a stampeding mustang at 7:00 am?"

I flushed. "Rhett, this is serious. Are the kids awake? Do you think Mr. Jim would mind giving us a ride to the bus stop? They're going to be late for school. I'm not sure what happened to my alarm this morning, but it didn't go off." My words were half apologetic and full of anxiety. Why I felt the need to apologize, I didn't know. I waited for the scolding to come. Why hadn't I checked my alarm? Double checked? I must have looked like the most irresponsible mother at this point.

Rhett grabbed my arms and looked at me, his smile gone and a concerned frown on his face. "Leia, stop. You didn't miss your alarm. I shut it off."

I stared at his gorgeous face in shock as his words began to register in my panicked brain. "What? But why? The kids are going to be late now!" I moved around him, sure now that the kids were in the kitchen with his chef and I would have to call the school before I received a call for their absence. But his hand stopped me.

"The kids are fine, Leia. I had Mr. Jim take them to school this morning. I figured you needed a chance to get some sleep and that maybe we could talk over breakfast this morning."

I gaped at him. He'd shut my alarm off? And had Mr. Jim drop the kids off at school? I felt dizzy.

"You had no right."

He cocked his head at my quiet words. The anger built in me. Who the fuck did he think he was? I'd known him less than a day and already he was coming into my life, taking over, and making decisions without even asking me if it was ok?

"I told you last night, these are *my* children. I decide what happens. And there is no *talking over breakfast*. This was a one-time thing. One time and that's it." Each word was punctuated with a step closer until my neck was craning to look up at him. "You might think you're some knight in shining armor coming to rescue the damsel in distress, but that's not me. That will *never* be me again." I stepped away, and he watched me with a stony expression. An unreadable mask settled over his handsome face.

"Thank you for your hospitality, Mr. Barrett. Whatever guilt you feel over Danny's death, you can check it off as absolved. Your debt has been paid."

A shadow passed over his face, but still he didn't give anything away. It wasn't until I'd turned away again that I heard his rich voice reach my ears.

"My debt could never be repaid."

I turned back. "Well, that's on your conscious, not mine."

His jaw clenched and his blue eyes hardened. "You're right. It is on my conscious. Do you know what Danny told me before he died?"

I pressed my lips together. To my knowledge, Danny had died alone, a mortar round striking his position and killing him instantly. "Danny was killed instantly."

Rhett shook his head. "Wrong. I got to him

before he passed away. And do you know what his last words were, Leia?"

Something in me began to crack and splinter. "Don't…" I whispered. But Rhett took a step forward.

"His last words were, 'Tell Leia that I'm sorry I couldn't be the man she needed. Tell her that I'm sorry she always had to do everything on her own. Tell her that I'm sorry I was a coward. Instead of stepping up and being the man she needed, I ran away. Because being a soldier was easier than admitting I couldn't be a husband and a father. That I wasn't ready for it. That I wasn't ready for her'."

I shattered.

The thousand pieces of glass that my heart erupted into, lodged deep within my soul as wounds and memories I'd buried deep down, rushed to the surface.

The last time I'd seen Danny alive, we'd fought. Before he'd told me he was deploying once more where I'd begged him to do something, anything, to help me. It was a moment of weakness and frustration where I had been so tired of being the one to make the decisions on my own.

Where I'd just wanted comfort and support. A partner and a friend.

He'd come home the next day and told me he was leaving on his next deployment. We never spoke of it again.

Tears streamed down my face. "You're lying." I whispered the words, but I knew it was wrong. I knew he loved our children, and me. But I'd always known deep down that Danny hadn't been ready to be a husband and father. I'd shoved the thought away so much and lived in such denial that I'd never seen how he'd struggled.

"You know I'm not, Leia. I was supposed to tell you at his burial, but how could I say that? How could I tell a woman who'd just lost her husband and the father to her children that he never felt worthy of that title?" He shook his head and ran fingers through his thick hair.

"When I saw you last night, my first thought was that maybe Danny had set you in my path because I hadn't delivered the message all those years ago." Blue eyes pierced mine. "But then I saw you with Jason and I realized it was something else. You think you want a hero? You had them with Danny and Jason. Both of them 'rescued' you and both of them let you down."

He gripped my chin and tipped my head back to look at him. "I told you I don't do charity cases, and I meant it. I take. I conquer. I win." his thumb grazed my trembling lips. "... I won't apologize for doing what needed to be done. I won't tell you I'm sorry for taking charge and making a decision." He stepped closer to me, pushing me against the wall and crowding into my space. "I'm not your hero, little lioness. I'm not a white knight. Fuck I'm not even a prince. I'm the man who will fuck you, break you, and then put you back together again. I don't need to rescue you, Leia because you don't need rescuing. But if you want someone who knows when to lead and when to call you out on your shit? Then maybe, just maybe, that could be me."

He dropped his thumb and walked away, leaving me standing with tears cooling on my cheeks and my mouth gaping open at his words. Words that had rocked my entire world.

Danny had always been good. But he'd never felt like he was enough. Jason had been good until he was bad. Both had come into my life when I desperately wanted a hero. A savior, because that's what I thought I needed. And Rhett was right. Both had let me down in their own way.

I watched him walk away and disappear behind a door to what I presumed was his own bedroom, before I turned and headed in the opposite direction toward the stairs that would lead down to the kitchen.

Rhett had been bossy and demanding from the moment I'd met him. He made decisions but always deferred to me. Except in this instance. I looked down at my phone and frowned. He'd turned my alarm off because he thought I needed sleep. He'd thought about *me*. Then he'd taken care of the one thing that would have worried me the most, my children. And he hadn't cared if I'd been pissed at him because in the end, he was right. I was exhausted.

I'd never had someone who looked after not only me, but what mattered to me. I'd never had someone lift part of the load for me without asking anything in return. Without making me feel like I was the burden to them.

Emotions and thoughts swirled in a confused whirlwind inside of me as I approached the kitchen and found his housekeeper, Pam, rinsing and loading dishes.

"Oh, good morning Ms. Leia!" Her cheery

voice was a bright spot in the dark cloud of my thoughts.

"Good morning, Pam. Is Mr. Jim around?"

Pam slid her gray eyes toward me and arched a brow. "Well, yes, he should be getting back any moment now from dropping the children off."

"Will he need to take Mr. Barrett anywhere today?" I refused to say his name. Keeping his formal title somehow put a safe cushion of distance between us. Because in saying his name, *Rhett*, it brought back memories of the way I'd moaned it last night. And right now I couldn't think clearly with his confession in my thoughts and the taste of him still on my mouth.

She shook her head and gave me a soft smile. "No, Rhett won't be needing Jim's services today. He only uses the car on formal business, but I believe he'd intended to drive himself to work this morning. He said that Mr. Jim was to help you with whatever you needed to do today."

At that moment, a side entry door opened and Mr. Jim stepped into the kitchen where he slid in next to Pam and gave her a kiss on the cheek. "Good morning, love! Children are all dropped off." He gave me a wink. "That Jameson is a good kid and Sarah can talk your ear off. You've raised some amazing children, Ms. Leia."

I smiled softly. "Just Leia, please. Mr. Jim, would you be able to help me with a ride today?"

He smiled back at me. "Of course, as soon as you drop the Mr. Jim" stuff. It's just Jim. Now, where did you need to go?"

I squirmed. "Well, to be honest, I'm not sure. But- have you ever heard of someone name Juniper Wild?"

Pam and Jim raised their brows and cast curious glances at each other.

"Yes, we know who Miss Wild is, but why would you need to find her?"

"Because I think she's the only one who can help me. Can you take me to her?"

Jim looked at Pam once more before nodding. "Of course, Leia. I know where she is, but are you sure you need to see her? Rhett has said you can stay here as long as you like."

Pam slid a mug of coffee toward me, and for a moment, the thought crossed my mind. Could I stay here? I shook my head. No.

As much as the thought and Rhett's' words had hit home with me, I wouldn't risk taking another chance on another prince. Even if he insisted that he wasn't.

"Thank you, both of you, but I need to do this on my own."

I felt a pair of eyes on me then, and I looked up to see Rhett standing at the entrance to the kitchen, watching me. He was dressed in an all-black, perfectly tailored suit that made his tan skin stand out and his black hair gleam. He nodded to Jim and greeted Pam with a kiss as he made his way into the kitchen. His words were for Pam and Jim, but his eyes never left mine, their brilliant blue piercing through me.

"My business dealings will take me out of town for the next couple of days. Once you drop Mrs. Morrow off where she needs to go, please begin packing up the house. We'll be heading back to Denver." And then he was gone. He didn't say goodbye. Didn't ask me again to stay or offer to help. He just left. Exactly like I'd asked him to.

A pain like I'd never felt before, encompassed me. Like the one beating shard of my heart had finally, at last, stuttered and stopped.

An hour later Jim dropped me off outside of a building that looked like it had once belonged to a historical society, not a women and children's shel-ter. I looked up at the bright yellow sign that read "Wild's Emporium" and turned back to Jim. "This is it?"

Jim shrugged and nodded. "So it says. I believe you can find Juniper in her shop inside."

I hugged my purse and nodded. Mr. Jim stood at my back, holding open the car door. "Do you want me to wait for you?" I could see it in his eyes. He didn't want to leave me here. To be honest, I didn't like it either. But I couldn't go back. I shook my head.

"No. Thank you, Jim, I'll be fine." I checked the time. I had about four hours before I needed to leave to meet the children at their school, and in that time I had to secure a place to stay, a car and maybe even a job. The thought was daunting. Could I get all that done on my own? Doubt crept in and just as I was about to turn around and ask Jim to stay, maybe just a few minutes longer, I saw him drive away.

Well, that was that. I was on my own.

Squaring my shoulders, I marched into the building and gasped in shock. The outside may have looked like it belong in an old western, but inside was truly a work of art. Old-fashioned storefronts lined a fake cobblestone street that made you feel like you were truly stepping back in time. The shops glowed with warm lights and flickering faux gas lamps. Inside each store were unique wares from artisans and vendors. Some shops even had small stands outside displaying a few of their sample wares.

I stopped by one and eyed a willowy woman with long, blonde hair and a beaded fringe head-band. Her dress was a crochet creation that somehow flowed around her in a kaleidoscope of colors. She was sitting at a small table littered with small crystals and a deck of tarot cards.

"Yes." She made it like a statement to a question I hadn't even asked.

"Excuse me?" Large eyes looked at me, and she gave me a soft smile.

"You were going to ask me if you'd made the right choice and the answer is, yes." She cocked her head. "Sort of…"

I blinked and shook my head. "I'm sorry, no, I wasn't going to ask that." Although I *had* been thinking about it. "I was going to ask where I could find Juniper Wild?"

"Oh! Well, that's even easier to answer. She's in her shop at the end of the street." The woman stood up to point in the right direction. "And the answer to your other question is also yes."

"I didn't even ask a question!" I stuttered, but she just put her hand on my shoulder and gave me a sympathetic look.

"Hun, you didn't have to. It's all over your face. You're in a tight spot and you're wondering if we can help. And the answer is yes, we can." She patted me comfortingly. "But your other question? Well, whether it's a 'yes' is really up to you."

"You aren't making any sense." I wondered if somehow I'd stepped into the Twilight Zone of antique shops and crazy, crystal-wearing fortune tellers. Next thing I'd know, someone would come around the corner trying to sell me snake oil.

She shrugged, apparently perfectly fine with the fact that she spoke in riddles and sat back down to shuffle her cards once more. "Come by when you're done with June and I'll give you a reading." She cocked her head, her eyes looking at something in the distance. "Or maybe don't. You might not have time." She blinked and smiled at me again before going back to flipping cards over one at a time, essentially dismissing me.

Baffled by her strangeness but also amused, I just shook my head and continued on my way until I stopped in front of a small storefront with a sign simply stating, "Juniper's Tattoo Gallery."

Opening the door, I was greeted by a cozy interior decorated with images of art in all mediums on the walls. Water colors, oil paintings, charcoal drawings and more. Pictures of mountains and wildflowers. Faces, people. Not at all what I would have envisioned in a tattoo parlor. In fact, it looked more like an art gallery posing as a tattoo shop.

Behind a half-wall partition and bent over the back of a burly man who was perched on her tattoo chair, the artist herself was busy at work. Her tattoo gun was in her hand, small ink pots and trays neatly arranged on a small, rolling cart beside her. She had a mask on so I could only see half her face, but I made out thick, dark lashes, pretty blue eyes, and a head of thick blonde hair she'd pulled back into a sloppy bun.

The shop wasn't the only thing that didn't look like they belonged. In fact, only the big guy with a thick beard and so many tattoos I wasn't sure there was even a square inch free to cover, looked like he fit the bill of someone that should be in a tattoo parlor.

"John, if you don't quit squirming, I'm going to end up spelling your new girlfriend's name wrong and I'm not sure you have another tattoo we can cover up to correct it."

John huffed and glared at the woman, who glared right back at him. "Well, couldn't you have picked a different spot? That close to the spine hurts."

She rolled her eyes. "I'm not close to the spine at all. It's on your shoulder and no, I couldn't because the last *three* spots I covered previously have been all taken. Maybe you could try keeping a girlfriend this time instead of just immortalizing her on your skin?"

John huffed and squirmed again but then settled down long enough for Juniper to go back to concentrating on her work. The buzz of the tattoo gun was the only noise in the shop and finally, after a few minutes, she sat back and pulled her mask down.

"Alright John-boy. We're all done!"

I got a glimpse of a sturdy oak tree and in the deep, inky-green and grays of the ink, I could see a name formed through the branches and leaves. Little birds and animals scampered on its bough and peeked out from among the leaves. I had no idea what the original tattoo was underneath, but the new one was stunning, both masculine and soft at the same time. I looked at the tattoo and then glanced at the artwork on the walls, and realized that the gallery images were all Juniper's.

Juniper turned toward me as John was admiring his new ink and attempting to take photos of it to send to his new girlfriend.

"Hey! Let me clean up and I'll be right with you. Warning, though, I'm booked solid for the next two months on custom pieces, but if you're just looking for a little flash, I have a folder on the table with some of my pieces."

She was young, younger than me probably, but there was a quiet confidence to her that instantly put me at ease and I returned her smile.

"Actually, I'm here about your foundation. The Wild One's? You help women and children in need?" I asked hesitantly.

"Oh!" Her eyebrows raised in surprise, but she nodded. "Of course! Give me just a minute." She turned back to John and murmured a few words about aftercare and then followed him out the door. "And John— try to keep this one ok?"

Then she shut the door and turned back to me with a warm smile.

"Do you like chocolate?" Her question startled me. I thought she would ask me about my situation and what help I needed. Not my sweets preference.

"Well, yes, I do…" She took off her mask and threw it in a little waste basket.

"Great! My friend Vy makes the *best* death by chocolate brownies you've ever tasted. Let's go." She opened her door and stepped out onto the main street and I followed, if not hesitantly, behind her.

"I'm sorry but, I thought you were Juniper Wild, of the Wild One's Foundation?" I asked as we wove our way through the shoppers who were coming in and out of the stores.

"I am."

"And why are we going to your friends for brownies?" Part of me wondered if maybe these brownies were a code for something else. Or maybe something else was *in* the brownies and that explained why the tarot card lady had seemed so cooky.

Juniper cast me a side glance and smiled. "Because you look like you could use some chocolate. And if you're here asking for help from the Wild Ones, then I'm probably guessing a regular brownie just won't do. So why don't you just come with me to Vy's and we'll see if we can help you solve both problems?"

I couldn't help but smile back and ended up following her without another word until we approached a small bakery storefront that had windows lined with mouth-watering treats. The door *dinged* as we entered, and a petite, dark-haired woman came from the back with a smile dimpling her cheeks.

"Vy, we have someone that could use one of your famous heartbreak brownies." Vy's warm, brown eyes lit up when she saw me.

"Of course! Come on back. I just pulled a fresh batch out of the oven." She turned around and led the way to a small kitchen where trays of heavenly chocolate confections were cooling on racks.

Vy grabbed a small plate and cut into the corner of a tray of brownies before handing it to me. "I hope you like corner pieces. They're my favorite."

I smiled and bit into the dark chocolate confection, my eyes widening in surprise. "Oh, my gosh. These are amazing!"

Vy smiled, her eyes dancing in delight. "Thank you! It's my grandmother's recipe." She waved a hand to a few stools that were tucked under the counter. "Come on, sit down and I'll make some coffee to go with that while you tell me and Juniper what we can do to help."

Just then, a voice came from behind us. "She doesn't really need our help, more like we need hers."

I turned to see the same fringe-wearing, tarot card fortune teller from earlier entering the kitchen, smiling at us and I immediately pulled the brownie out of my mouth, giving it a suspicious look.

She snorted and shook her head, the fringe dancing. "It's safe to eat. Vy doesn't believe in the medicinal use of herbs in her baking, although I've told her time and time again she's a witch in the kitchen." She gave me a wink and picked up her own brownie before taking a bite. "I'm Lacey, by the way."

Juniper pulled a stool out for me and motioned for me to sit. "Alright, well, we will deal with Lacey's rather vague statement in a bit. First things first. What's your name and what can we help you with?"

Lacey waved a hand and marched behind the counter to help Vy with the coffee. "I already told you. We can't help her, but she can help us."

Juniper cast her friend an annoyed look before turning back to me. "Ignore her. She thinks she can see people's futures based on their aura."

"I *can*, Juniper Wild, or did you forget about that time I told you that you were going to get into an accident and a day later you did?" Lacey huffed while Vy ignored the both of them and carried over a steaming mug of coffee, placing it down next to my brownie plate with a wink and a look that said she was used to their banter.

"You said I might want to avoid being in the rain for a bit, which is a *normal thing* to avoid, and the next day, I happened to slip in a puddle outside the Emporium and fell on my ass."

Lacey's eyebrows raised and gave me a look as if to say, 'See! I was right.' before turning back to Juniper. "A puddle that was there *because it had rained that morning.*" She waved a coffee spoon in the air to emphasize her statement, and Juniper shook her head in exasperation.

I cleared my throat. "Well, umm…I don't know anything about auras or fortunes, but I know Lacey is wrong. I *do* need help."

Three sets of eyes turned toward me with sympathy.

Vy came and sat down across from me, folding her hands around her coffee mug. "Oh hun, all jokes aside. Why are you here?"

And with a deep breath, I began to tell my story to three women I'd never met before, but somehow knew they were going to be the key to my freedom.

CHAPTER 11

LEIA

Forty-five minutes later, after spilling nearly my entire life story to strangers, I held my palms out to them and sighed. "And there you have it. I have nothing left to my name anymore. Jason put everything in his, including the only vehicle we had. I haven't worked in years but I know I can get a job. I have to. I just need a place to stay and a start."

Juniper spoke first. "And what about this Rhett? It sounds like he was more than capable of helping you get back on your feet, not to mention the *other things.*" Her eyes twinkled. "Not going to lie, if a man offered me all that after just one night, I'm not sure I wouldn't tie *him* down in his sleep."

I chuckled. At first I hadn't been sure how much to share with the women, but their presence was soothing, or maybe there was something in the brownies because before I knew it I'd opened up not only about Danny, Jason, and the situation I was in, but Rhett too.

"Well, other than knowing he owns a pharmaceutical company, I don't exactly have a way to contact him." I frowned. "And honestly, I'm not sure he wants me to. He's probably regretting everything already."

Lacey raised a blonde brow. "Girl, first of all we need to get you out of this self-depreciating talk. This man gave you the best *multiple* orgasms of your life and promised to do more, and you think he's regretting it? Check your phone."

"What?" I was confused. "Why should I check my phone?"

"He's ex-military, and he turned your alarms off. I happen to know a thing or two about some military guys and based on what you're telling me, I think I know exactly the kind of unit he was in. Check your phone, I bet he left a way to contact him just in case."

I pulled my phone out of my purse, confused

and disbelieving, but opened up my contacts, anyway. Sure enough, there was a new one. He'd left me his cell phone number with a note containing one word, "muffin". He hadn't asked me or waited for me to ask him. He'd just done it. A thrill went through me. Never mind how he'd managed to unlock my phone. I'd deal with that little fact later.

I put my phone away.

"Okay, so he left his phone number, but that doesn't mean I can call him up for help and honestly, I don't want to. I need to do this on my own." I drained the rest of my coffee and Vy got up to refill it. I smiled my thanks and continued on. "So, can the Wild One's help? How does this work?"

Lacey and Juniper cast nervous glances toward each other, but it was Vy who spoke as she set my mug back down with another piece of brownie. "Well, unfortunately Lacey is right in this instance. We can't help you, but you can definitely help us."

I frowned in confusion and disappointment. "What do you mean? I thought you guys were a resource for women and children in my situation with no place to go?" Immediately I began wracking my brain for new ideas and solutions. I started to stand, grabbing my purse and things.

Juniper looked at Vy in confusion, and Lacey grinned. "See! I knew it." She blinked and wrinkled her nose. "Ok, but, how is she going to help us? That part I didn't see as clearly…"

Juniper frowned at Lacey. "I thought you said you knew!"

Lacey sipped her coffee and smiled over the rim. "I said I knew she could help us, but I didn't see the *how*."

Vy rolled her eyes. "Ladies, come on. Focus here, Leia needs our help still, even if we can't provide all the resources she's asking for. We can still come up with a plan, and I think I have one."

All of us were paying attention now.

"Okay, Leia, you said you used to work at a marketing firm, correct?"

I nodded. "Yes, and I loved my job but, it just wasn't as fulfilling as I thought it was going to be. Then Danny died, and I felt guilty about not being around as much for the kids. So I gave up my job to stay home with them and don't get me wrong, I love my kids but I loved working too."

"Okay and what do you think *would* fulfill you?" Her warm, brown eyes bore into mine, searching me as if she knew the answer before I did.

I was quiet for a minute and then slowly, an idea began to take shape. "Honestly, I'd love to help women just like me. Women who feel lost and alone in the world. Woman who just want a better life and a fresh start." Something shifted inside of me and I felt a rush of warmth. As if my whole heart and soul was saying this was right.

Vy nodded, her eyes dancing with excitement. "Yes. Women who have been kicked in the balls by life but get back up swinging every time. Women who want something to fight for, live for, and call their own."

I grinned. "Yes! Women who don't want to be rescued, but who just need a chance to find their purpose in life and create their own happy ending."

All three women looked at each other and grinned. Juniper turned to me. "I think I know what Vy is saying. Leia, how would you like to come work for the Wild Ones Foundation? We need someone with passion and vision to help spread the word about our work. And with your skills in marketing, I think you're the person who can get it done."

Lacey spoke next, "We have all the funds ready to go. There's just so much red tape through the state and so many hoops to jump through that it's delayed some of the progress. We've only been able to help a few people but want to do so much more. It's why we can't offer you shelter or anything more than support right now. The building we want to buy, the land we want to purchase is all tied up in red tape and beurocracy."

Vy huffed. "It's so frustrating. And people in this city are so suspicious of anything new that they don't want to help us. But if we had someone handling the marketing and getting our name out there, we know we can reach so many more women and help so many. We just don't know where to start."

Excitement like I hadn't felt in a long time bubbled up, but was quickly tempered with reality. I shook my head. "Guys, I love this idea and would love to help, but it still doesn't solve the current problem. I need a place for me and my kids, like yesterday, and a job that pays. As much as I would love to say yes, I just can't. I'm sorry."

I hated seeing their crestfallen faces and for a moment, I thought it was going to be the end of our conversation. Standing up I offered a sincere smile. "Thank you for listening to me. This was probably the first time in a long time that I've felt like I had some girlfriends to vent to, even if we just met. You have no idea how much I needed it. And the brownies were absolute magic, Vy. You definitely have a gift." Grabbing my purse I turned to go. I only had a couple more hours to come up with a new plan.

"Wait!" Juniper stood up, knocking her stool back. "I think I have a solution."

Arching a brow, I turned back to her as Vy and Lacey looked at her with matching confused expressions, and Vy stood up to fix the stool. Juniper didn't even notice as she came around the counter, bouncing excitedly.

"There's a small apartment above the Emporium. It used to be an office, but there's a kitchen, a living space and two bedrooms. I was eventually going to turn it into the headquarters for the Wild Ones Foundation but you need it more. What if you stayed there?" She turned back to Vy.

"And Vy didn't you say you needed help on the weekends with the front counter, so you can bake more? What if Leia worked here part time?" She looked at Lacey. "And you as well Lacey. You were just saying you needed help with bookings and packaging orders."

Juniper turned back to me, her blue eyes dancing. "Lacey was right. Crazy, but right. We can't help you Leia, but you *can* help us. This project is too big for us to manage our businesses and the foundation on our own. We need you."

I cast my gaze over the women, their expressions full of excited hope and felt an overpowering sensation of gratefulness. It could work. As crazy and as unexpected as it was, I knew in my soul that this could work. I grinned.

"Ladies, say hello to the Wild Ones Foundation's newest marketing manager."

An hour later after excitedly discussing schedules, when I'd start work and how we'd proceed, Juniper had led me up a set of stairs that were hidden in the back of the building to a small, two-bedroom apartment that had clearly been converted into an office space at one point. If the faded green carpet and striped wallpaper said anything, it had probably not been touched since the late eighties. But I didn't care. It had everything we needed and I couldn't wait to pick up the kids.

Lacey and Vy said they'd help me get it cleaned up, and I decided I'd use some of the kids college funds to buy what we needed to furnish it. And soon enough I'd be earning money toward paying it all back.

After saying goodbye to the ladies, I took the bus for what I promised myself would be the last time to Sarah's school, where I'd already called and arranged for Jameson to be dropped off so I could pick them both up at the same time.

After being buzzed-in through their security doors, I walked into the front office of the school. l I looked around for two blonde heads that should have been waiting for me, but didn't see them. Frowning I approached the front counter and the secretary that was sitting at a desk behind it.

"Hi, I'm Leia Morrow, are Jameson and Sarah Morrow here?"

The middle-aged woman glanced up at me with a frown. "Well they were, but they're gone now."

I froze. "Excuse me?"

The lady cocked her head and then glanced

down at a sign-in sheet. "Yes, it says that they were picked up by their father, Jason Rodgers?"

My fingers gripped the counter, and I swayed as a wave of dizzying fear swept over me.

"You, you let them go with him?" My voice shook, and the woman stood up, bringing the sheet with her.

"Yes, he's on the approved pick up list. Was there an issue?" She looked at me with genuine concern.

"He's not their father. He was my fiancé, my ex-fiancé. I completely forgot to remove him from the approved pick up list. There wasn't time."

"Oh no. I'm so sorry. Should we call the police? Are the children in danger?" She moved back to the desk and picked up the phone to dial, but I stopped her.

"No! No, I'm sure they are fine. There was just a miscommunication. Thank you." I turned to go.

"I'm so sorry Mrs. Morrow. We will remove him from the approved list right away." I gave her a grim smile before rushing out of the school.

My phone buzzed, and I looked down at it.

Jason: I'm sure by now you know where the kids are.

Ready to come home yet?

Me: You had no right.

Jason: Don't be like that Leia. Just come home and let's talk.

Me: Do not touch my kids. Do you hear me? Do not touch my kids.

There was no response, and fear gripped my heart. But I knew Jason wouldn't hurt them. He was doing this for one reason and one reason only.

To get to me.

Fear turned to rage. That motherfucker.

I was done with his manipulation and his lies.

It was time to let him know he'd pushed me too far this time.

Instead of waiting for the next bus, I searched my contacts for someone who might help. One name stood out to me.

He picked up on the first ring.

"Yes?" His voice was low, rough, and at the sound, warmth flooded through me. Had Jason ever picked up on the first ring for me? I honestly couldn't remember.

"Rhett, when you said that you would help me, did you mean it? No strings attached?"

There was a pause, and I heard a shuffle of movement as if he was shifting in a chair.

"The only strings I would attach to you, Leia, are the ones I had you in last night."

Heat flushed through me at the insinuation.

"Well, umm, good— because I kind of need your help. Can you send Mr. Jim to pick me up from the kids' school?"

He didn't hesitate. "I can do one better. I'll be there in five minutes."

"No! No." Something in me didn't want to bring him back to Jason's apartment. This was something I needed to do myself. "Just send Mr. Jim if you can. I just need a ride and the bus will take too long."

There was another pause. "What aren't you telling me, Leia?"

"Rhett…" my voice was a pleading whisper. "I promise. If I need you, I will call you." I licked my lips and finally said what I'd been thinking since the morning. "Thank you for this morning. For letting me sleep and making sure the kids got to school. I've never had someone do that for me before and I didn't know how to handle it. I'm so used to doing everything on my own that having someone help me felt like an intrusion. It felt like I was failing at my job as a mom and I didn't know how to handle it."

He was silent for a moment, and then he sighed. "I understand, little lioness. More than you can know. Jim will be there soon."

I smiled. "Thank you, Rhett. And thank you for leaving me your number."

He chuckled. "So long as you use it when you need it."

And then he hung up, and I was left staring at the phone. He didn't string me along. Didn't flirt or tease. Didn't guilt me for being unappreciative. He just did exactly as he promised to do.

"Soon" apparently meant lighting fast, because the next thing I knew a familiar Cadillac SUV was stopped in front of me and Jim was calling my name.

It was time to take back control.

CHAPTER 12

RHETT

I hung up the phone and shifted uncomfortably in my seat.

This was perhaps the hardest thing I'd ever done in my life. The urge to get up and rush to her was so overwhelming that sweat was breaking out across my brow, and my stomach was in knots.

But I had to trust her. I had to let her handle this on her own, for both her sake and mine.

Leia didn't need another hero. She didn't need to be told she was made of glass. Leia was pure steel. She needed a king to the queen that she was. And I knew without a shadow of a doubt she was the queen to my king.

My lioness.

I settled back into the deep leather chair, once

more in control of myself and my emotions. Whatever Leia needed, I knew Jim would handle it and alert me if the situation became dangerous.

The man behind the desk I was sitting across from was studying me in the way a predator watches another predator. His dark eyes glinting nearly black in the dim light of his office. Red underlights cast an eerie glow over the plush, black carpet and deep mahogany wood of the sleek floor-to-ceiling cabinets and bookshelves. It had been surprising to see the shelves were lined with actual books as well. Most men who were trying to display their wealth and power didn't pay attention to what books went on their shelves, or even read half of them.

But this man had clearly picked the books himself, and by the looks of their spines and worn covers, they were well read. I recognized some of the names and titles, Marcus Aurelius, Seneca, and Epictetus to start. The Stoics. Greek philosophers who founded a philosophy of teachings based off logic, physics and ethics. Next to them was a well-worn copy of Sun Tzu's "Art of War". Without speaking a word, Kage Diovolo had revealed everything about himself that I needed to know.

This man was as dangerous as any I had faced across a battlefield.

And I could trust him.

He spoke first. "I'm not used to someone dealing with other matters while conducting business with me. That must have been personal."

Kage was probing. Trying to see if I'd open up and share with him, testing to see if I'd reveal a weakness. I had no weaknesses.

"It was." Two words. That's all he needed to know. Business or not, I would stop everything, stop the world if needed, to take care of what was mine. And Leia was most certainly mine.

"Hmmm…" He cocked his head and the gold skull earring that dangled from his left ear, the only indication that he was more than just a CEO meeting with another CEO, glittered in the low lighting. A slow grin spread across his face and he leaned forward, folding his hands on top of the desk.

"I like you, Rhett." It was like saying a wolf liked red meat.

"I'm not here to earn your approval, Mr. Diovolo. I'm here to find out where my product is and get it back." Gauntlet thrown down. The game was on.

A black brow raised and the grin widened. "I'm not sure what you mean. I've never had any dealings with you, or your pharmaceutical company, until now. And if you're insinuating that your missing product was somehow illegally obtained by anyone in my company," his grin was full of sharp teeth while those souless, black eyes flickered with veiled menace. Wolf indeed. "...well that sounds like a dangerous accusation."

I studied him, keeping my face impassive and not letting the threat and hint of violence in his voice rattle me. After a breath of weighted minutes, I let a wolfish grin of my own split my lips. "It would only be an accusation if I didn't have proof."

I reached into my inner suit pocket pulling out a small, red plastic bag containing two small, blue capsules with a grinning skull stamped on the front of the plastic and tossed it onto his desk. "That was purchased at one of your clubs recently."

He picked up the bag and looked at it and the contents the barest of seconds before returning his gaze to me. "I have many clubs, Mr. Barrett, and I can't control or be responsible for every activity that goes on in them. This is hardly proof of anything."

"That bag was sold at your own, *personal,* club, Mr. Diovolo." I sat back and watched as his grin turned into a frown. "Pothos" *is* your private club, yes? An exclusive, invite-only getaway for Denver's elite?" Pothos wasn't just a place for the elite. Named after the greek god of sexual longing and desire, it was an appropriate name for a club rooted in hedonism. Whatever you wanted, whatever you longed for, Pothos could deliver. And it delivered in a way that could never be traced back to the person who made the request.

"You're correct, Pothos is invite-only. I don't recall ever extending you an invite." There was a bite to his tone now. Kage didn't like his personal retreat threatened.

I cocked my head. "You didn't."

The bomb I just dropped made Kage sit back and reevaluate me differently. No longer was I a pushy businessman trying to corner him. Now I was a threat. I'd just revealed that I had effectively and efficiently infiltrated his impenetrable fortress without so much as a blip on his radar. I could already see the wheels of his mind spinning, evaluating his associates and making connections. He wouldn't find any, however.

"Don't start the interrogations just yet, Kage. You'll just end up killing off beneficial associates at the expense of secrets that they didn't spill." I reached out and picked up the bag off the desk where he'd dropped it and held it up to the light.

"I had my lab analyze the drug that is being sold and distributed at your private little getaway. My company has spent a long time researching and developing a new treatment for alzeimer patients. It is unique and the chemical compound make up is easily identifiable. By itself, it's a fairly harmless drug. But combined with the right narcotic? It's a potent high. More euphoric than any street drug currently. And also deadly."

When the warehouse had first reported a shipment of the experimental medication missing I'd initially thought it had been a competitor. But then strange overdoses had begun showing up and their toxicology reports were flagging the unique compound in our drug.

"This is laced with it. It's also unlike anything you currently have on the market. These pills are new, different, and I don't think you even knew they were being sold right under your nose." I twirled the package in my fingers before slipping it back inside my jacket pocket as I leaned forward, letting him see my earnestness now.

"You're a lot of things Kage Diovolo, but above all else, you're a businessman. You'd never let a product you didn't have direct control over be sold right under your nose. Especially one that caused a high rate of death and could lead the feds right to your door."

Kage's fingers, covered with grinning skull tattoos, tapped rhythmically on the top of his ebony walnut desk. He was quiet for a moment while he gathered his thoughts, those black eyes never leaving my face.

Finally he spoke. "You'll need to give me time to investigate."

It wasn't an admission of anything, but it wasn't a get the fuck out at the end of a gun either. I nodded. "Understandable. But I would suggest you hurry your investigation as quickly as possible. And when you find the culprit? I want to be there." It wasn't a question. I wanted to see the fucker who had jeaporidzied my companies credibilty and dared steal from me.

His eyes narrowed, "And I want to know how

the fuck you got into my club without my invitation."

I smirked and stood. "You're just a man, Kage Diovolo. Not everything is under your control." My eyes flicked to the works of Marcus Aurelius and Kage followed my gaze before he tipped his head back and let out a barking laugh.

"Fine. Point taken. I'll let you know when I have information to share."

Leaving his office I checked my messages for an update from Jim and shot off a message letting him know I was on my way to relieve him. It was time to show my little lioness that I was one man wouldn't let her down.

CHAPTER 13

LEIA

The drive to my old apartment was a short one. Thankfully, Jim didn't ask too many questions and agreed that he would wait for me.

This wouldn't take long. I would go in, say what I needed to say, grab a few of my things and the kids' items and then we'd leave. And I'd make sure that Jason understood in no uncertain terms that he was never to contact me or the children again.

I wasn't sure what to expect when I opened the door, but it certainly wasn't the sight that greeted me.

The apartment was spotless. There weren't any signs of our fight or the hasty way we'd left.

In fact, it was clean, tidy and there was a delicious smell coming from the kitchen and dining room. I heard laughter and frowned in confusion. I'd expected to see Jameson and Sarah sitting on a couch, nervously waiting for me to come and get them.

Instead, when I rounded the corner, I was greeted with the sight of both children laughing across the table from Jason. A board game spread out between them. I cast a quick glance around, wondering if I was seeing things. The kitchen was just as spotless as the rest of the apartment and on the stove it looked like the source of that delicious scent was dinner being made.

Sarah was the first to notice me and she jumped up with a squealed "Mommy!" coming over to give me a big hug.

"Look at what Papa Jason brought us!" She pulled me towards the table where Jameson was frowning in concentration over his next move and Jason was smiling at me with a hopeful, innocent expression.

"Hey baby, why don't you sit down and join us on the next turn? Dinner will be ready in just a few minutes."

I stared at him in disbelief and then shook my

head. "No. I'm not staying." I looked at the chil-dren and could see their faces become crestfallen. "*We're* not staying. Guys, go grab your backpacks and anything else you want from your rooms. I need to talk to Jason for a minute."

Sarah and Jameson gave each other a look and then slowly backed away from the table before going to do what I'd asked. I said a silent prayer of thanks that for once they didn't argue with me or complain, and then I turned back to Jason.

"What the fuck is this?" my voice snarled.

Jason stood up. "Leia, baby, come on. I'm trying to say I'm sorry here."

I snorted. "By picking up my kids without talking to me? Buying them a game and making dinner? Did you really think I'd just walk in here and forgive everything?" I shook my head and turned to leave, but he stopped me with a hand on my arm.

"Look, just talk to me. Just listen to what I have to say and then if you want to leave, you can."

Arching a brow, I looked down at where his hand gripped my arm and felt nothing but disgust. Jerking my arm away I saw that Jameson and Sarah were standing in the livingroom, their backpacks stuffed full and their arms filled with belongings. Their eyes were wide and worried as they watched us. I turned back to Jason. "Fine, but in the bedroom. The kids don't need to hear any more of your lies."

He followed me back to the bedroom and shut the door. I crossed my arms and waited.

"Why are you being like this, Leia?" I frowned.

"Excuse me? Jason, you *cheated* on me. With our neighbor, who is barely what, nineteen?"

"She's twenty-one." He frowned, and I scoffed.

"Oh, like that's any better. You know what? I don't want to hear what you have to say. I just want to get my things and go. Never call me or try to contact the kids again. And if you *ever* pull a stunt like you did today, I will put a restraining order on you." I moved past him to the door, but he stepped in front of me.

"I knew you were going to be a bitch about this. All I tried to do was pick up the kids for you and make a nice dinner to show you I'm sorry for what happened. Heather was a one-time thing and nothing even happened. *She* came on to me.

But did you even ask if I did anything with her? No. You just assumed the worst."

My eyes widened in shock. Was he really going to turn this around on me? A small part of me cowered at his words. The part of me that was used to him blaming me for everything and convincing myself that he was right and I was wrong. But no more. I narrowed my eyes and stepped closer to him, my finger shoving into his chest.

"Get out of my way, Jason. I'm not going to say it again."

"Or you'll do what? You're pathetic, Leia. You always have been. I don't know what Danny saw in you. He wouldn't stop talking about you like you were God's gift to men. I used to listen to him talk and think that someone like you shouldn't be with a pussy like him. What could you possibly have seen in a guy like that? But now I know. You're just as pathetic and useless as he is." The viciousness of his words was like bullets ricocheting off the walls of my mind.

"What the fuck Jason! Danny was your best friend. How could you talk about him like that?" I couldn't believe what I was hearing from the man I'd believed to be my dead husband's best friend.

Jason scoffed, his lip curling into a disgusted sneer. "Danny was a loser, and I never felt more than relief that he was finally shut up for good. Always bragging about his amazing family and you. About how he was going to go home and try to be a better husband and father. Well, guess who went home? Me. Not him. And guess who stepped in to be the man he could never be? Me."

Bile gathered at the back of my throat as memories of Jason showing up at the funeral. Smiling. Caring. Helping. Playing with the kids. It was like the gaping hole that was left by Danny's absence was filled, partially. I'd never questioned why. I'd never thought that I needed to.

"You fucking son-of-a-bitch." My hand flew without me realizing it and then next thing I knew, Jason's head snapped back as I'd punched him as hard as I could right in the nose. Before he could react, I brought my knee up between his thighs, connecting with his balls. He dropped like a stone, his scream of pain like music to my ears.

I stepped over his writhing body and opened the door, not bothering to look back or even go back to gather any of my items. There was no need. I wanted nothing more to do with lies I'd been living and the narcissistic asshole who'd kept me carefully trapped with them.

The kids were staring at me wide-eyed as they rushed toward the door at the sound of Jason howling. I hushed them and rushed them toward the front door.

Making it down to the ground floor and outside where Mr. Jim was still waiting, I stopped short, expecting to see the older gentlemen still there. But he was nowhere to be found.

Instead, there was a black Lexus IS sedan with a tall figure in an Italian-cut, all-black suit leaning against the car. At our approach, his head snapped up, those gorgeous aquamarine colored eyes softening in relief.

"I was going to give you two more minutes before going up there."

I smiled, something squeezing in my chest, and a warm feeling settled over my shoulders. I knew what it was now. Danny. It was his presence I felt any time I was near Rhett. Something I'd never felt around Jason.

"It was nothing I couldn't handle."

Rhett nodded, his eyes darkening as he moved toward me and I didn't miss how he carefully scanned me and the kids, looking for any signs that we weren't ok. "I know. But I was here just in case." He cocked his head, a dark brow arching as a smile played over his full lips. Lips I desperately wanted to kiss again.

"So, we missed out on a trip to the ice cream store yesterday. Are you up for a trip now?"

I looked down at the kids who were staring at me with hopeful expressions and then I turned back to Rhett.

"On one condition."

He eyed me curiously. "Ok, what's the condition?"

My lips curled up in a teasing grin as I leaned forward and whispered something in his ear.

Rhett tipped his head back and roared with laughter. A sound that sent thrills through me.

"Alright, little lioness, if it's a muffin you want. It's a muffin you'll get." His gaze was full of dark promise as he leaned in and kissed me, not caring that the kids both made gagging noises as they stood next to us. "But you're going to have to choose a new word now. Because I think this one has a new meaning."

I grinned and let him lead us to his car, and as I did that feeling of a warm embrace slowly slipped away from my shoulders and unraveled itself from around my heart. I thought my heart had been made of glass. I thought it had been shattered into a million tiny pieces. But in reality, it was just locked away, waiting for the time when I realized I didn't need a prince or anyone else to save me.

But a handsome, kinky, fairy godfather would do instead.

CHAPTER 14

RHETT

My eyes didn't need to adjust to the darkness. I was used to the shadows. It was where I worked best. Where I felt most at home.

Finally, I could strip the trappings off my outward billionaire, CEO appearance and be who I truly was on the inside. Cold. Calculated. Ruthless. A killer.

The two men on either side of me were cut from the same cloth. All of us with different backgrounds and reasons for being here. But all of us are bound by one simple code. Protect what is ours and destroy our enemies.

We didn't speak as we waited for the man who was gagged and bound to a chair to wake up. A man I'd hunted ruthlessly for years. He'd hid his tracks well. So well that it had taken a random and completely by accident meeting, for me to realize he'd been my target all along. Rage at the years he'd gone unnoticed and spreading his poison all this time flared to life once more.

If I hadn't stopped in the store. If I had just driven by and saved my inspection for another day, another time. How long would it have continued?

I'd never suspected he was the cause of so much pain and heartache either. He'd been an oily rat from the moment he'd become a part of my unit and fallen under my command. But he had always been just slippery enough that I couldn't kick him out and send him packing. And when I'd come back to the States and had begun investigating what had happened on that last mission; why Danny had died so needlessly, he'd already safely entrenched himself with his new host. Danny's widow.

My Leia. *Mine.*

I didn't feel any jealousy or guilt over the past and Danny. I'd known him well enough in life to know he wouldn't begrudge how I felt about her. Or what I'd do to protect her.

The man stirred finally. He groaned and then as his eyes opened up and he realized he was trapped; they widened in fear and he began to struggle.

I stepped forward into the dim light of the workshop we were in. The floor was cold concrete and all around us were sheets of thick plastic, hung to protect the rest of the space from anything that might accidentally escape.

"Hello Jason."

Jason blinked in surprise, then his eyes narrowed in anger. I could tell he wanted to speak, so I ripped off the duct tape that had covered his mouth, not caring if skin pulled away with it.

He cursed and spat. "What the fuck, Barrett. Why am I here?"

I smiled and knew it wasn't pleasant. "I think you know."

His face turned red. "Is it because of Leia? You're coming at me like a psycho because of some pussy?"

Darkness creeped the edges of my vision and I had to resist the urge to kill him right then. "No, Jason. It's not because of Leia. Not entirely, at least. It's because of Danny."

I knelt so that we could be on eye level, so that I could see the realization that he'd finally been caught, spread across his face. I wanted to savor this moment. Savor the exact second that he realized justice had come for him.

His eyes widened until I could see the white edges as my words sank in. "Barrett, Major…" he stuttered, while using my rank to appeal to me. To appeal to the bond of brotherhood I once thought we'd shared, on some level at least.

"You said Danny came under mortar fire." I cocked my head, watching as all the blood drained from his face. "But you know something funny? Our intel team said there weren't any mortars in the area. And then it was confirmed by the satellite later on. So how did he die, Jason? You were with him on that mission. You were his teammate. Tell me how he died."

Jason sputtered as he tried to pull together some semblance of bravado. "Fuck you, Barrett. You weren't there. You were too busy getting all the praise and 'attaboys' from command, while me and the guys were out there doing all the fucking dirty work."

"Wrong, asshole. I *was* there. I was there when Danny died. I saw the wounds. I heard his last words. But you know who wasn't? *You.* Because like the filthy rat you are, you took off back to the bird and booked it out of there, claiming you'd been *wounded.*" I stood and looked down on him, snarling the words as they left my mouth. "You killed him. And then you staged it to look like you'd come under mortar fire. Don't even try to deny it. It took me a long time to finally figure it out and put the pieces together, but when I saw you with Leia, I knew the truth."

"I'm not saying shit. I want a lawyer." He narrowed his eyes at me and tried to sit up taller in the chair. I almost laughed.

"Look around, you shithead. Does this look like a fucking court house?" I watched as realization dawned on his face.

"You aren't going to kill me." His voice shook, and I grinned.

"You're right. I'm not." His shoulders dropped with relief.

Behind me, the two men who'd been standing in the shadows stepped into the light. Men, I'd only recently met but knew immediately they were the type of men I'd want next to me in a battle.

"You see, I'd almost given up looking for you, Jason. But then my warehouse here had informed me that there'd been a security breach and that an experimental drug we've been holding until it clears FDA approval, was stolen." I circled around him and he craned his neck, trying to watch my movements.

Kage spoke, his voice as cold as the grave. "Not long after, Mr. Barrett contacted me and let me know that he'd found his drug being sold in some of my establishments. At first, I thought he was trying to move into my territory." He stepped forward and stared at Jason with unblinking, coal-black eyes. The dim light glinted off a gold earring as he tilted his head, silently observing. "And that's when Mr. Black here came to me with some information about a guy he knew who was selling drugs to the bikers who frequented his shop. Bikers who were ending up dead."

The other man crossed his arms over his chest, the skulls and smoke tattoos that decorated his skin moving in a way that it looked like the skulls were yawning, screaming their death.

I picked up where Kage left off. "So no. As much as I'd like to be the one to rip your heart out and feed it to you. I'm not going to do that. Because they are." Jason started to blubber, and I watched with satisfaction as his jeans darkened and the unmistakable scent of urine filled the air.

"Bro, please no…I didn't know I was moving in on the Diablo's. I didn't…Rhett, Sir, Major Barrett!!"

But I was done listening to him. I stepped back into the shadows as Kage stepped forward and commanded Jason's attention.

"Do you know what this is?" He held up a cell phone and smiled. The cold way his lips spread across his face reminding me of the same skulls that decorated Cade's arms. When I'd first met Kage, he'd not been what I expected. Instead, he was more business-like and calculated than I'd thought the president of a biker gang would be. Cade, even though he seemed to have taken a step away from the inner-workings of a motorcycle gang, had been surprisingly ruthless. It had been his idea to use his workshop, stating that he wanted to rid the trash that was infecting his city, himself.

Jason's wide eyes darted between the two men, but he was too scared to speak.

"You're a bomb guy. So I'm just going to lay it out for you. This little device will transmit a signal to a bomb. A very tiny, very *discreet* bomb. Can you guess where the bomb is?"

Jason squirmed, his panicked eyes trying to discern where it might be hiding.

Cade rolled his eyes. "It's in your ass, dipshit."

Kage glanced at his friend, one dark brow arching slightly as the only sign that he was mildly annoyed. "You ruin everything."

Cade frowned and shrugged. "Sorry, you were taking too long and I need to get this place cleaned up before the shop opens."

Nodding, Kage returned to Jason and held the phone up again. "Rhett informed us of how you killed your friend, so I thought it would be poetic justice if we did the same. Only we're much kinder than you were. You have a chance to escape your fate." He moved a few paces away.

"When the phone finishes ringing, the signal will be sent to the bomb. Pretty fitting for the kind of guy you are, right? A literal hole is about to be blown in your ass." He hit the dial button and then placed the phone on the floor. "Get to the phone in time and maybe you'll save yourself." He grinned and then turned to walk away. "Or maybe you won't."

Both men followed me through the thick

curtain of plastic sheeting as we heard Jason grunt and topple his chair over, scooting with all his might to reach the phone.

The explosion happened in the next seconds. Blood and matter splattering against the plastic as the three of us watched.

I wanted to smile as I wondered what Danny would say about this moment. But I didn't. The moment felt too somber, as if Danny was finally at rest. His last words had been for Leia. There'd been no mention of the man who'd killed him. He'd never known about the betrayal that was coming for him or the coward who had harbored so much jealousy toward him. My eyes slid to Kage, who actually *was* grinning in a macabre way, almost as if he was enjoying himself. "Remind me not to let my pharmaceuticals get on your streets again."

Kage chuckled. "Remind me not to fuck with your friends." We watched a severed hand slide down the sheeting.

"Remind me to buy more bleach." Cade grumbled.

EPILOGUE

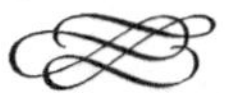

LEIA

Strong hands glided over the globes of my ass, molding and massaging them with a firm and demanding touch. I sighed softly and snuggled deeper into my blankets and pillows while keeping my breath even and shallow, as if I was still in a deep sleep.

I felt the rough glide of his unshaven jaw against my cheek and then heard the low rumble of his still-sleepy voice in my ear. "Shhhh…keep pretending to be asleep baby. I want to fuck you awake."

Those same strong hands left a trail of heat over my skin as they traveled up my thighs, over the soft slope of my belly and up to my chest where they cupped my breasts, gently kneading their fullness as he pulled me closer to him. His hips arched against me, the thick length of him sliding between my thighs and I bit back a moan. He'd said to be quiet and I had an extra reason to obey him. The kids were sleeping in their room just next door and the walls of the tiny apartment were paper-thin.

It had been several months since I'd moved into the run down apartment above the Emporium but in that short time I'd made it our home. Rhett hadn't said a word about the threadbare carpet or the second-hand furniture. The only thing he'd insisted on was an updated security system that of course he had the code to.

Something I'd discovered when he'd slipped into my bed one night soon after installing it, and had proceeded to wake me up just like the first night we'd spent together. How he'd managed to secretly install straps and bindings to the head-board and footboard, I still didn't know and he wouldn't tell me. Not that I cared when he was sliding that thickness oh so slowly inside of me, stretching and filling me with a delicious ache that I couldn't get enough of.

He rocked into me, slow and deep, the pace his to set, his to control, and that alone set me over the edge even before his fingers found the sweet bundle of nerves that had me crying into my comforter. Rhett followed me into bliss soon after as he slammed home deep inside of me. We stayed locked like that for several heartbeats as the sun started to peek through the drapes, casting a warm glow over the room.

My body sated and secure in his strong arms, I felt myself begin to drift back into sleep until a soft knock on the bedroom door and Jamesons voice on the other side startled me wide awake. "Mom? Are you up?"

I sighed and sat up with a quick glance to the alarm clock. Technically I didn't need to be up for another twenty minutes, but ever since Rhett had told Jameson that he'd take him to boxing lessons if he focused more in school, the boy had been getting up and ready without me asking for weeks now. The incentive had worked too, it seemed, because three nights a week Jameson went to lessons and with every one I'd seen his confidence and his grades improve. When I'd asked Rhett how he knew that Jameson would like boxing he'd smiled and told me that it was something Danny had enjoyed too. They'd often work off some steam in a makeshift boxing ring, just the two of them, after a long or strenuous mission. I hadn't known what to think of that and had felt a little remorseful that it was something Danny had never shared with me. But in the end I could see how happy it made Jameson, and I was glad he had something of his dad to connect with.

"Yes, I'm up. Be out in just a minute." I called out to him before swinging my feet over the side of the bed and casting a look over my shoulder at the man who was watching me with hooded, lust-filled eyes.

"I think you should let Jim take the kids to school this morning." He grabbed my hand, forcing me to stay put. I cocked a brow and gently pulled my hand away.

"We've talked about this. Mr. Jim has more important things to do besides run my errands." I stood up and he grabbed my hand again, tugging on it gently until I tumbled back into the bed and into his arms. Before I could squeak out a "Rhett!" he'd flipped and pinned me to the bed where he hovered over me, his hips pressing into mine.

"Let's try this again. Leia, will you please let Jim take the kids to school today?" His tone was light, but there was something to his gaze that made me pause my immediate retort of "no.", and study him. My eyes traced the dark shadow on unshaven face before meeting the serious, blue eyes that were watching me just as closely. My heart sped up.

"Why would I let Mr. Jim take the kids today?" I frowned, a thousand worried thoughts going through my head. Was something wrong?

A smile curled at the corner of his lush mouth before he lowered his head to kiss the tip of my nose. "You're adorable when you jump to the worst possible conclusions."

I gasped, "I do not—!"

"I want Mr. Jim to take the kids to school because I'd like to spend the rest of the day making love to my fiancé."

"Fiancé? Rhett, what are you talking about?" I struggled and pushed against his chest but then I felt something slip onto my hand.

"Of course, you have to say yes first, Leia."

My eyes widened as I lifted up my left hand and stared at the ring he'd placed there. A gorgeous, round diamond framed by a halo of sapphires glinted in the morning light. Warmth filled me from the soles of my feet to the top of my head and before I could say a word, tears burst out of me.

"Leia? Baby?" Rhett's worried tone broke through the bubble of sobs, snot and emotion that overcame me. He pulled away and pulled me up, his words tumbling over themselves as I continued to cry. "Leia I'm so sorry, I shouldn't have sprung this on you like that. I should have planned it out better…" He stood up and ran his hands through his messy, dark hair as he pulled on a pair of sweats and then handed me a robe. I sniffed and took it absentmindedly while still staring at the ring on my hand. "I'll go make some coffee.", he muttered and opened the door before I could say anything else.

I sat there for a moment, staring at my hand, replaying his question over and over in my head. The answer resounding over and over in my mind. So why couldn't I say it? Why couldn't I get the words out of my heart and past my lips?

Finally after what seemed like an eternity, the sounds of breakfast being made and hushed whispers reached my ears. I slipped on the robe to make my way to the kitchen.

Three sets of blue eyes turned toward me expectantly. Rhett stood in the center of the small kitchen with a mug of coffee in one hand and a spatula in the other. He was smiling softly, not a hint of anger or frustration, or even worry in his gaze. Whatever decision I made, I knew in that instant, he would respect it completely. A familiar warmth filled me again. The same feeling I'd gotten when he'd first convinced me not to take the city bus to the hospital all those months ago.

"Mom?" Sarah's voice pierced my thoughts and my gaze found my children watching me, waiting expectantly for something and I realized that they were waiting on me. On my answer. My eyes found Rhett's again and he answered my unspoken question.

"I talked to them before I even bought the ring." He was completely unapologetic.

"When?"

"About a week after you moved in here."

I whirled on my kids who were grinning from ear to ear. "You guys kept this from me this whole time?"

Jameson rolled his eyes. "Duh, mom. So? Did you say yes?" Sarah stepped up next to her brother. "You *are* going to say 'yes', right mom?"

I grinned and turned back to Rhett who was watching me, his face a guarded mask. "It's ok

Leia, if you're not ready, you're not ready. I'll wait." His eyes said it all. He'd wait. He'd wait forever for me. I could choose my own ending, my own story, but I knew that my story wasn't complete without him in it. This was my ending. This was my happy ever after.

I gave the answer my brain, my soul, my entire being had screamed at me the moment I'd seen him standing behind me in the pharmacy line.

"Yes, Rhett Barrett. A thousand times, yes."

The End

AFTERWORD

Thank you so much for reading Heart of Glass! What started out as a short story for an anthology turned into a one of my favorite book couples ever. I fell in love with Rhett and Leia, so I hope you did too! If you enjoyed the book I'd love it if you could share your thoughts or even just a star with a review. Reviews are the second best way to support an author's work. The first is by word of mouth! If you enjoy any of my books, please share with your friends and others. Thank you so much! Xoxo- Anne

ACKNOWLEDGMENTS

As always, I want to say thanks to my amazing family for supporting me on this journey. To my real-life hero and husband, I love you so much. Thank you for being the Rhett to my Leia.

To my Muffins. Erica, Mandy, Michelle, and Kelly. Thank you for being the ears I needed, the solid and steady support and the encouraging words. I would have given up so many times if it wasn't for you ladies.

To my author mentors, Amelia H. and Debbie C. - I'm beyond thankful for your incredible support and friendship. Your knowledge of publishing has helped me become a better author and writer. I couldn't have done it without you.

And to my readers. You guys are amazing!! The way you support and hype me up keeps me going. Thank you for everything. Xoxo- Anne

ABOUT THE AUTHOR

Anne Roman is the author of suspenseful, 'edge of your seat' romance. She loves to write exciting twists and turns that leave her readers begging for more. When not writing you can find Anne playing Uber driver to one of her four children, hanging out with her hunky husband, or catering to two very spoiled cats and one spoiled dog. Want to get to know her? Join her Facebook group here:

Anne Roman- Romance on the Edge